WILD LOVE

JUNIPER SPRINGS BOOK 1

MELISSA SCHROEDER

Edited by
HEIDI SHOHAM AND NOEL VARNER
Cover Art by
SCOTT CARPENTER

HARMLESS PUBLISHING

Copyright © 2021 by Melissa Schroeder

All rights reserved.

No part of this book may be reproduced in any form or by any electronic or mechanical means, including information storage and retrieval systems, without written permission from the author, except for the use of brief quotations in a book review.

❦ Created with Vellum

To all of those who kept our country going through the pandemic. Thanks to all the doctors, nurses, respiratory therapists, hospital staff, and essential workers in grocery stores, food delivery services, and gas stations. You kept our country running while putting your lives on the line. We will never be able to repay your, but you are always in my thoughts.

CONTENTS

1. Everly	1
2. Quinn	13
3. Everly	25
4. Hawthorne Brother Text Thread	33
5. Quinn	35
6. Everly	43
7. Quinn	55
8. Everly	65
9. Quinn	75
10. Everly	85
11. Quinn	95
12. Everly	103
13. Quinn	113
14. Everly	123
15. Quinn	135
16. Everly	145
17. Quinn	155
18. Everly	163
19. Quinn	171
20. The Hawthorne Brother Text Thread	181
21. Everly	183
22. Quinn	195
23. Everly	201
24. Quinn	209
25. Everly	217
26. Quinn	227
Epilogue 1	233
Epilogue 2	245

Acknowledgments	259
The Melissa Schroeder Instalove Collection	261
About the Author	263
Also by Melissa Schroeder	265

1

EVERLY

I'm almost thirty years old and I believe in one truth in the world: Some shit goblins just deserve to be dick punched.

Case and point, Jacob Warren, the shit goblin presently smirking at me. He stands surrounded by all his other man boys—aka fan boys, but of the manly sort who hate women for being strong—his condescending smile telling me that he thinks he put me in my place. And why would he do that? Because he's a man and I'm a woman. That's it.

I'm a lot of things. A sister, definitely a fighter, a best friend, and lover of all things dark and caffeinated. I'm definitely not someone who keeps her feelings to herself.

Ever.

"Excuse me?" I ask, my voice quiet and dark. It's what my brother Mason calls my death voice.

Out of the corner of my eye, I see a few of the other convention attendees take a step back—especially the men. They've dealt with me before and know better than to say stupid shit like this shit goblin is spouting. And yes, I know I used the word shit twice in a sentence and I have used the term shit goblin multiple times, but these are desperate times. This is a professional conference, and I can't hit a man for being an asshole or I won't be invited back. At least, that's what they said last time I did it.

"I said you're successful because of the oddity. You know there aren't a lot of women in this business, so people show up for the weirdness of it."

He owns a little—and I mean *very* little—bookstore in the Dallas area. This is not the first time I've had to deal with him and definitely not the first time I have had to deal with the attitude.

I feel my fingers curl into my palm, as my anger soars. Once lit, my temper can burn anyone in my path to the ground. The need to dick punch him almost overwhelms all me. But I hear my brother Wyatt's voice rumble through my mind.

Use your words, Evie, not your fists. It takes me a few seconds to battle back the rage, but I do it.

"Actually, Jakey," I say, loving the way his lips curl into a snarl at my use of a nickname. "My partner Becca and I have found out that we're not that much of an oddity." I see a few women in the audience of onlookers nod their heads. "Yes, we're a minority in the industry, but we aren't an oddity. If I remember correctly, you told my partner Becca we would fail in the first year when you tried to convince her to dump me and work for you."

His nostrils flare. He's always been an asshole. Average height with dull brown hair, little beady eyes, and the most ridiculous soul patch. He's a hipster through and through and has the overpowering cologne to prove it. And he doesn't have to make a living at this. It's his hobby since his family is big in the oil and has been for generations. He knows next to nothing about how to run a business, but he never fails to tell me what's wrong with mine. See, he *is* a shit goblin who mansplains and I think we can both agree that they are the worst kinds of shit goblins.

"Is that what she told you?"

I laugh. "Oh, yeah, but the best part was listening to you beg her."

"I did not."

"Yeah, when you started in on her, Becca started recording the interaction." One thing about my bestie and business partner Becca Gold: People think she's flighty. She is, but she's sharp when it comes to our shop, and both of us have learned how to handle men in the business. Also, she didn't really record it, but she did tell me about it. He doesn't need to know that.

"Becca is—"

I see the malice in his eyes. My smile fades as I step closer. "Be very careful. I controlled my temper before now, but you say something about Becca, I will not hesitate to make you cry in front of your man boys."

His little soul patch quivers. "I'd expect nothing less from someone of your background."

Someone gasps and I want to laugh again.

"That's fine, Jakey. I might come from a working class background, but Becca and I are still kicking your ass in sales. Oh, and writers and artists like us more than you. I mean, did Stan Lee travel to your store?"

I know he didn't, but Lee wanted to see our store not too long after we opened. We proudly have a picture of the three of us in the store.

Warren opens his mouth to argue, but nothing comes out. For what seems like a lifetime, he stands there, his mouth hanging open, his eyes narrowed and threatening, but still, he says nothing.

Finally, he snaps his mouth shut. With a huff, he turns on his heel and stomps off. Good god, what an idiot. His man boys following his wake, but I have noticed that the number of his man boys is decreasing from year to year so that's at least something.

There is a smattering of applause and I take a bow. "Thank you."

As people come up to talk to me, a tickle forms in the back of my throat. I have never been good with big crowds, and definitely not when I'm being touched. Not in a bad touch kind of way, but someone with anxiety issues and just this side of the spectrum, I don't like being the center of attention.

"Well, this has been fun, but I have to call my business partner."

A few people try to gain my attention, but I hurry off to the bank of elevators as I avoid making eye contact with anyone. Sweat is already gathering at the base of my neck, a sure sign I'm nervous. It takes less than five minutes before I'm in my hotel room and I'm tossing my bra on the bed like every woman does the moment she gets a chance.

The sigh that escapes fills the silence in the room. That alone blankets my soul, even as my body is still reacting to the interaction downstairs. My mind is still racing, my heart feels as if it is ready to escape through my throat. Panic attacks aren't always normal for me. I know I am a weirdo because confronting Warren was less stressful than the people who wanted to talk to me after he ran away. It's just the way I am and I no longer apologize for it.

Okay, I will be honest. I've never apologized for myself at least since I turned eighteen. But, still, I sometimes wish I was different. I wish I was like Becca who had no problem with crowds and hated to be alone. Life would probably be easier for me if I was, although I know that my bestie has her own issues.

Grabbing my tablet, I call her. I know she should be home by now. Her face comes on the screen complete with a big smile. I instantly feel the rest of my anxiety leave my system. We've been friends for so long, I don't know what it's like to not have her to calm me down. Between her and my brother Wyatt, I've learned to control my issues.

Her smile fades. "What happened?"

I sigh, knowing I can't lie. Becca can always figure out when I'm not being truthful.

"Warren."

She rolls her eyes. "Tell me you didn't hit him again."

"I did not. I threatened to, but I did not."

She claps. "Good for you."

This is where I have to explain something about my BFF Becca. Raised for the first third of her life by a single mother who was also an artist, she views the world with hippie rose gold colored glasses. Where I'm doom and gloom, she's rainbows and unicorns. Seriously. She sported rainbow hair years before it was the cool thing to do.

Happiness pours out of her soul and brightens the world around her. Yeah, this is definitely a best friends who are total opposites kind of situation. But she believes in positive reinforcement. She gets that from her mother. The two of them are always the brightest people in any room.

"It was hard because he deserved the dick punch. He said that our success is due to our tits."

She gasps in true Becca fashion. "Not true. Quite the opposite."

"I pointed that out. Then I pointed out we kicked his ass in sales and Stan Lee came to our store and not his."

"Good. Although, next time, maybe I will just dick punch him."

I chuckle because it will never happen. Becca isn't a pushover, but she's sweet. Her mother raised her to be a pacifist, which is interesting since her stepbrother is in the military.

"I wish he would just go find another hobby. I also wish you could be here."

She nods. "Yeah, but with Flint heading back to California tomorrow, I couldn't go."

"I know."

Her oldest stepbrother is a SEAL who has to return back to his base. Knowing that he could be deployed at any time, it was understandable that Becca wanted to say goodbye.

"I'm still so proud of you."

"Thank you."

Then she frowns. "I should be there with you."

"What?"

"I should be there. I spent a lot of time with Flint and he would understand."

"No. You are spending time with Flint and we both know how important family is."

We both missed out on a normal childhood thanks to our situations.

"I know, but you're family too."

"Who will be back in a few days. You won't see Flint for several months. That's more important."

"So you are still staying a couple extra days?"

I nod. We had planned on taking the time for a mini vacation but life intruded. "I need to blow off some steam."

"Of course," she says with a roll of her eyes. "How can we forget about your vajacations?"

Our town is tiny, a speck of dust on the giant Texas map. I learned not to have affairs in town. There's no way to avoid the guy no matter what. Nerdvana, our store, sits on Main Street, so everyone stops by, even if they aren't into comics or manga. Can you imagine having a one-night stand and then having to deal with seeing the guy constantly? No thank you. Plus, the small-town life is definitely ripe for gossip. I usually don't care, because I live my life on my own terms, but I don't like answering questions. Or dealing with messy emotions.

So, I take vajacations—vacations for my vagina. I had wanted to call them fuckations, but Becca said that would offend people. I don't care as long as I get laid and since

I'm in Denver at a bookseller's convention, I feel the need to mingle hitting me. I mean, not to talk to people. Just sex. With one dude, not a bunch of people. That sounds like a nightmare to me.

"Are you ever going to get sick of one night stands?"

"Never." Although I say it with more conviction than I feel. Lately, my trips and the men I hook up are getting a little…tedious. I would never say that out loud, because if I'm getting bored, I have no idea what that means. I haven't wanted to get involved with a dude since college and that debacle.

I push all thoughts of Trent the Asshole out of my brain.

"So, tell me what the Golds are doing tonight?"

"We're going to The Mason Jar. Flint claims he can't find good Texas bar-b-que outside of the state."

I make a note to text my youngest brother—the Mason of The Mason Jar— to tell him I'll cover the bill. It's the least I can do.

"Well I need to shower the scum of this convention off my skin, and then I'm going out. I vote we stop coming to these things."

She frowns. "I should have come with you." I know she's worried about me, but I need to make sure she understands what I mean.

I shake my head. "You need to spend time with Flint. I just don't know what these things do for the business. When we first started out, they really helped us. But now…"

"Yeah, I think we might need to look at presenting at some of them."

And just like that, a rush of spiders dance down my spine. "Wait, what?"

She smiles into the camera, her aquamarine eyes sparkling. "Don't panic. I'll handle the panels, but it would give us more exposure."

"Eh, not sure that's important."

"Everly LuluBelle Spencer."

"That is *not* my middle name."

She knows, but she comes up with insane middle names for everyone.

"You're the numbers bitch of the two of us and know that it will help us."

You know the worst thing about Becca? She's smart and she has no problem telling me that I'm wrong. And I know she's right. The more exposure we get the better, especially in the day of digital books. "Fine, but I will not be the one doing the panels."

"Fine."

There is a small beat of silence where we stare each other, then we both start laughing. Yeah, that's as bad as we fight.

"Tell Flint to be careful," I say.

She nods. "Love you and text me when you are safe and sound."

"Will do. Love you."

Once we click off, I flop back onto the mattress. I want to forget about that conversation, but I have one of those brains that zeroes in on my insecurities. I've gotten better in the last few years, but it's still there and the idea of being one of the presenters is enough to make me break out in hives.

Yes, Becca would do the presentation, but everyone knows we're a team. That means people will want to talk to me about the business. And sometimes, I can do it, but when people are looking at me like I know what I'm doing—it's enough to make me want to freak out. I do know what I'm doing. I kick ass, but I have a fear of failure.

I close my eyes and do my relaxation exercises. Thanks to therapy along with yoga instruction, I've gotten much better dealing with my anxiety. Thankfully, I have nothing else scheduled for the rest of my trip. I have tonight, and all day tomorrow, then my flight is noon the next day. The relaxation is important.

So, I take my time getting ready. The shower is long and steamy, so hot I almost scald my skin. But I need it. This has been a long three days of meetings, panels, and discussions. The Comic and Graphic Books Convention is one of the bigger ones and is always in Denver. I love this town, so I'm always up for coming up for a visit. An hour later, I'm slipping on a pair of jeans, a t-shirt that reads *Looking for Trouble? Look no Further*, and my favorite pair of Chuck's. I apply an extra topping of lip gloss and inspect myself in the mirror. *Not bad, Everly.*

I glance at the full sleeve that covers my right arm. The color explosion there represents the important things in my life. Nerdvana, Becca, my brothers. Captain Marvel's shield...along with Thor's hammer. I know I need to start on the other arm, but I haven't figured out what to do there. Part of me wants to put Elliot Danvers the anti-hero of *Glass Edges*, the futuristic graphic novel series by Q. Hawthorne. But for some reason, I haven't been able to come up with a definitive idea, so I wait.

With one last look in the mirror, I grab my phone and head out for the night. Convention time is over and it's time to find a man to use for the night.

2

QUINN

I stare out the window at the blackness past the security lights around our family vacation home in Colorado. There's nothing like nighttime in Colorado. I like the quiet, the stillness of the mountains. Sometimes, I just need this, everything to be calm and easy.

"That's what you're wearing?" my youngest brother Carter asks, as he walks across the great room. He's wearing a pair of dress slacks and a button-down shirt that matches his green eyes. Right now, though, he's giving my t-shirt, jeans, and Chuck's a dirty look.

"Yes."

He settles his hands on his hips that makes him look a lot like our mother when we were younger. I'm not sure he would appreciate that observation, but knowing Carter, he would take pride in it so I keep it to myself.

"Why? I'm trying to help you here, brother. I can't get you laid if we don't get you in proper clothes."

"Proper clothes? I think you don't know sex works.

Clothes are not needed. In fact, it's definitely better without them."

He rolls his eyes.

"But you have to get a woman first."

"I don't need a woman."

He eyes me. We all hate when he does this. He's a pain in our asses, but he is insanely perceptive. And I don't want to get into my recent dry spell. And by dry spell, I mean Death Valley looks like an ocean compared to my recent sex life.

"Maybe we can find you a woman who is into the whole disillusioned artist look you have going on there."

"Carter, leave him alone," our older brother Gavin says as he walks down the stairs. The only married one of out of the four brothers, he's also the calmest. People always think his twin Grady is the calm one, but he's just always waiting to explode about something. Gavin is serene as usual as he grabs the keys.

"Where's Grady?" Carter asks.

"Taking care of Syd."

That's Grady's executive assistant who accompanied us on this trip. She's had a migraine the entire trip, but Grady has other reasons.

"Let's do this!" Carter yells.

"Shut the hell up, Carter," Gavin says with little heat as he hurries us both out of the door. "One thing about migraines is loud noises can cause more pain."

Carter turns to go back into the house but we each grab him by an arm.

"What the fuck?"

We drag him to the rented SUV, then release him.

"You were about to go into the house and yell sorry. That is the opposite of what I told you to do."

Carter says nothing to that and yells, "Shotgun!"

We ignore him as we both get into the Escalade.

I slip into the backseat and wonder just that the fuck I'm doing here. Not in the SUV, but in Denver.

Avoiding work.

That's what it is. I've blown past two deadlines, and I am seriously in trouble of losing my publisher.

"Get out of your head, Quinn," Carter says. "Tonight is about drinking and woman. Well, for us. Our married brother will just text his husband." He points to Gavin.

I roll my eyes, but look out at the dark abyss of nighttime in Colorado. Our family owns a massive estate in the mountains outside of Denver, and we made a trip of it while our oldest brother and twin to Gavin, Grady, is here to get the family's newest venture going. They all work for Hawthorn Enterprises. I'm the lone weirdo, too entrenched in his art and stories to add anything to the coffers. Not that they need me.

"So, what's the over/under that Grady finally makes a move on Syd?" Carter asks.

"Carter, if you don't want me to tell Mom about your comment, I would dial it back," Gavin says.

"Psh, Mom worked for Dad in the early days, just like Syd works for Grady. He's been half in love with her for over a year."

That much is true. I think it's more that Syd doesn't put up with his crap. Grady is accustomed to women falling all over him. As his executive assistant, Syd keeps everything straight for him, including him. I mean, the pheromones when you are in the room with them can give anyone a contact high. And now they are staying alone tonight at the estate because Sydney had a really bad migraine.

"What do you think, Oh Silent One?" Carter asks.

"I think it's none of your business."

"I think it's all our business because it will affect the business. I just don't want him to screw it up."

"If there is one thing Grady knows how to do, it's planning," Gavin says. As fraternal twins, they are the closest out of all of us.

"Not always good in romance. Look at you," Carter remarks. "You almost didn't bag Oliver and that was with Captain America's help."

Oliver is my brother's husband and my agent. And yes. My asshole brother calls me Captain America, mainly because he knows next to nothing about my work. I knew the moment I met Oliver that Gavin and him would do well together. Gavin is too straight-laced, and well, Oliver isn't.

We turn on to I-25 and I see the lights of Denver up ahead of us. Thank god because after the plane ride up here, the trip up to the house, and now this drive, I've had about enough of Carter. I love him, but he never shuts up.

"So, our goal is to get Quinn laid."

I don't take my gaze away from the approaching lights. "I did not agree to that."

"You need a woman. At least for one night." Carter says it as if he's some kind of expert on the subject.

"And why would that be?"

He turns back to look at me and I pull my attention

away from the scenery. I notice that Gavin—the one brother who usually doesn't put up with any of Carter's crap—isn't saying anything to stop this. *Way to abandon me, big brother.*

"When was the last time you drew or wrote? Before the divorce, am I right?"

I look out the window again. I never thought I would be divorced, but I should have seen it coming. Abby thought that being married to a graphic novelist would be fun. It isn't. Just like any other writer, I have my issues. Most times I would rather be at home writing or drawing. Definitely not hanging out in Manhattan with socialites, but apparently, she thought that was what our lives would be like. I was never really like that while we were dating so I have no idea where she came up with the idea.

"Listen, Quinn." Carter snaps his fingers. I hate when he does that to me. I narrow my eyes and glare in his direction. "Sexual happiness is important to the creative process. It's been almost two years since your breakup and I'm pretty sure it wasn't going right to begin with."

"Why do you say that?"

"Abby was never a woman I would put with you. She was too hard." He waves his hand in front of his face. "Anyway, a night in the bed with the right woman might just put you back on track. Take it from Dr. Carter."

"You aren't a doctor."

"I'm a doctor of loooove."

I roll my eyes and look at Gavin who has remained silent. "Any comments."

Gavin sighs as he glances up in the rear view mirror. "I hate to admit it, but he might be right."

"Of course I'm right."

"Shut up," Gavin says. "But he is right. You need a night to blow off some steam."

"Did your husband suggest this?"

"Absolutely not. Oliver says not to meddle with the genius."

"But?"

He pulls into the parking lot of the club. "I'm your brother. I know you better than he does."

As he parks the SUV and steps out, a valet rushes forward to take his keys.

"Worse thing that can happen is that there is no woman you want to bed in here and we have some good drinks," Carter says with a smile. "Plus, I want to check this place out."

Carter's role in the family business is beyond the television area. He works in live entertainment and is in the middle of expanding our brand into night clubs.

"Sure, but you're buying."

"Always. Mainly because I can write it off."

Asshole. But he isn't wrong. This is work for him. We make our way into the club, and immediately, I regret coming. It's so damned loud. The pounding rhythm of the music threatens to crack my skull open. Why do people like this? I glance at Carter who is bobbing and weaving through the crowd. Of course, he got us into the VIP room.

An hour later, I'm only on my second whiskey. It's definitely the type to sip, but I'm bored out of my skull. Gavin is indeed texting with Oliver, and Carter has been dancing nonstop. He's always been like this, though. His

ADHD can drive me nutty, since I am the exact opposite.

All of the sudden something catches his eye, and he turns toward the bar against the opposite wall. Usually, I ignore his antics, but the moment I see the dark-haired woman he approaches, I can't tear my gaze away. I can't see her that well this far away, but she's definitely not his usually type. Carter goes for the girly girls, the ones who use a mirror as much as he does. This one is dressed in a t-shirt and jeans.

Carter motions in my direction and she looks where he is pointing. The breath backs up in my throat and my heart starts beating so hard I can feel it everywhere in my body.

She's goddamn beautiful. Not made up, but one of those dark beauties, with smooth skin. Her eyes look dark, but I can't tell this far away. I notice she has some ink on her arm. She shakes her head at Carter and turns back around to the bar. He looks back and sees me. He shrugs, then motions for me to come down there.

"You better go, or he'll just drag you down there."

I glance at Gavin. He's still looking down at his phone, but he didn't miss the interaction. Not much gets by the lawyer in the family.

"Tell Ollie I said hi," I say as I reluctantly head out of the VIP area. It takes me a moment or two to make it across the floor. There is no way to go around the edges. The dance floor is raised, with no walkways on the side. I'm sure Carter will say it's shit design and he wouldn't be wrong.

"There he is," Carter says smiling at me.

The woman glances over her shoulder, ready to dismiss me, then she goes completely still.

"Everly, this is my brother Quinn. Quinn, this is Everly. She's from Texas too."

She turns to face me, her gaze sliding down my body. By the time she makes eye contact with me again, my entire body is buzzing and my dick is definitely happy at the attention.

"Nice to meet you, Quinn," she shouts.

"Likewise."

Her mouth twitches.

"My work here is done. I need to go talk with our other brother. It's going to take me forever to get back up there. Shit floor design. It was very nice to meet you," he says, then gives me a pointed look. Fuck, he's going to want some kind of payment for finding the one woman in the sea of clubbers, who is probably a good match.

"So, your brother's your pimp?" she asks, leaning closer but still having to talk loudly to be heard over the music. She has one of those sassy Texas accents that I love. It wraps around the words and dares people to mess with her. I like it. And her. I like her a lot.

I chuckle and lean against the bar, my entire body humming for the the first time in forever. "He's been worried about me. I have no idea why he can't just leave me alone."

"Exactly! I have people always saying things like, you should get out more, Everly. Don't dick punch chauvinistic bastards, *Everly*."

"I disagree with that comment. Every chauvinistic bastard should be punched in the dick."

The driving beat of the music slows down, and a Shawn Menendez ballad comes on. As she downs the rest of her whiskey, I take her hand.

"Excuse me?"

"Let's dance."

"Uh, didn't I just tell you about the dick punch thing?"

"Yeah, but before you say yes to letting me fuck you, I thought we should at least dance, first."

"You're sure of yourself."

I chuckle again, because I haven't always been, but something about her makes me bolder. It's like I know we'll be magic together.

"Nope, but I'm trying to hedge my bet."

She hesitates, then a sexy, full on smile curves her lips. Her resistance dissolves as she allows me to tug her onto the dance floor. I take a few steps and then pull her into my arms.

As we dance, the rest of the crowd disappears. I slid my leg between hers, pulling her even closer. There is no way I can hide my erection, and I guess that I don't give a fuck about that. Even with the loud music I can hear her sharp intake of breath—or do I feel it? Not sure, but either way, it pushes my body into overdrive. My once dormant sex drive ratchets up and I know that I will do anything to get her beneath me. Or over me. Anything because for the first time in a very, very long time, I know what I want.

We return to the bar area and we both order whiskeys. The noise level makes it hard to talk. I lean close enough so she can hear me.

"Do you want to get out of here?"

Everly leans a little away from me, her gaze searching mine for a second. "On two conditions."

I nod, waiting for her to tell me what she wants.

"Only one night."

I blink. I don't think I have ever had a woman sound so adamant about that. It's no judgment on my part, but her determined tone tells me this is beyond important to her.

"Okay. And the second?"

"Are you sure you're okay with that first one? You have hearth and home stamped all over you."

My mouth twitches. I love this woman's chutzpah. "Yeah. I'm sure. What's your second condition?"

"And no personal information beyond our first names. I don't want to know what you do for a living, and I really don't want you to know how I earn my money."

That was oddly specific, but at the moment I would promise her just about anything to get her back to a hotel room. Fuck, I would grab a bathroom at the club truthfully. Need is still humming through me. My almost dormant libido has come roaring back to life and I need this woman now.

"Okay."

She eyes me skeptically. "Just like that?"

I nod then lean closer again. "I want to be inside of you, Everly, and I will do just about anything to get there."

She steps away and panic hits me square in the chest. Fuck. I don't want it to end like this. I don't understand the force that is urging me to take this woman to bed, but there is something there, something primal.

Then, she downs her whiskey, slamming the glass down on the bar.

"Okay, Quinn, let's go."

I down my drink enjoying the burn as it slides down my throat. She grabs my hand and starts pushing through the milling crowd. With the blaring music, there is no way I can hear what she is saying, but I know she is probably bitching. It makes me smile. As we finally make it to the front door, my phone buzzes in my pocket. I pull it out knowing it's probably Carter.

Carter: *I take it that you're off for the night?*
Me: *Yes. I'll get a car to take me back tomorrow.*
Carter: **huzzah-gif**
Me: *Stop.*
Carter: *Never. I am always right about women. Have fun, and wrap it up.*

Ugh. Fuck. I don't have condoms. I know we were out for the night, but I didn't think about that.

Everly is tapping on her phone and I realize she's getting a ride share car.

"We're going to have to make a stop."

She blinks up at me and even in the dim light, I can see the golden flecks buried in dark brown of her eyes. "Why?"

I like her so much. Most women would want to know why, but most would not be to just ask me about why.

"Condoms."

Her mouth twitches. "Really? God, you're cute." She

rises to her tiptoes and kisses me. It's over before I can really respond.

"Cute?"

"Do you know that at least five guys came up to me while I was at the bar and every one of those losers probably had condoms in their wallet?"

Fuck. She's making me blush.

"Oh, God, I'm going to have so much fun corrupting you."

I slip my arm around her waist and pull her closer to me, her back to my front. There is no hiding my erection. I take her earlobe between my teeth and tug on it. She shivers.

"I can promise you, I'll let you do just about anything to me as long as I get a taste of your sweet pussy."

Another shiver and she's pulling her phone up to type something on it.

"What are you doing?"

"Texting the driver. I want to make sure we can stop off at a drug store before we get to my hotel."

"Tell him there's a fifty-dollar tip involved."

3

EVERLY

The door to my hotel room slams open as we stumble over the threshold. Neither of us pay attention to it, or anything else. His hands are in my hair, his mouth on mine, and if I don't get him inside of me right this minute, I might explode.

Since we stepped onto the elevator, our hands have been all over each other. I just can't get enough of him. His hands slip down my body, grabbing my ass as he lifts me off the floor. Oh, god, he's amazing. As he slips his tongue along mine, he gyrates his hips, and there is no doubt how aroused he is. Of course, I've been feeling that from the moment we stepped onto the dance floor. He's long and thick, and I can't wait to have that monster inside of me.

He tosses the pharmacy bag on the nightstand as he carries me over to the bed—an amazing feat because I am not a small woman—and sits down, settling me on his lap. I swivel my hips and he leans his head back with a groan. I take advantage of our position and attack his throat. He smells of expensive whiskey and sexy, sweaty man.

"You're going to make me come in my pants, woman."

Power surges through me. My head spins as if I drank five bottles of whiskey in the last ten minutes. I giggle—actually giggle—but he frowns at me. Before I know what he's about, he stands up, taking me with him, then tumbles me back onto the mattress.

He has quick hands, I'll give him that. My shoes and socks are off my body before I can blink. Next, he's clawing at my jeans and I smack his hands away so I can take over the job. Once I have them unbuttoned and unzipped, he tugs them down my body along with my panties as I tear off my shirt and bra. Soon, I'm laying there completely naked. His eyes darken as his gaze roams down my body.

"Jesus," he says, reverence in his voice. I know I'm in good shape, but I have always thought I was too angular. Apparently Quinn does not.

"I don't think we need a third tonight, and definitely not part of the holy trinity."

His gaze shoots to mine then a smile moves over his face. It's possibly one of the most beautiful things I have ever witnessed. He has one dimple, on the right side, and he has these eyes, green rimmed with gold, and I can't seem to look away from him. And why would I want to. He's beyond gorgeous. Not movie star gorgeous like his brother. No there is a rugged quality to Quinn's features, from the carelessly styled hair, the big shoulders, and god...my gaze travels down to the outline of his cock. I bet that is as beautiful as he is.

"What?"

My gaze shoots up to his and he's frowning at me. I shake my head because it's super weird. I mean, I don't get inside my head during sex. I just feel, that's the best way to handle it. But this guy I barely know is tugging at my emotions and I have no idea why.

I smile, not wanting to freak out my one night stand.

"Nothing, just wondering how I got so lucky tonight."

"Funny. I've been thinking the same thing. I mean..." He waves his hands motioning toward my body as he licks his lips. Okay, I might have just died. "Fuck."

For the first time in about ten years, heat rushes to my face. I can't believe I'm blushing. I mean, lying here naked doesn't embarrass me. Still the appreciation in his voice and his expression is doing funny things to my insides.

"Thank you, sir. Sadly, I cannot give you the same admiration."

"What?"

He looks genuinely confused which makes me laugh.

"I want you naked too."

His expression lightens, another smile moving across his mouth. My heart turns over—a completely cliche thing for it to do. He drops down to his knees without taking his clothes off.

"What are you doing?"

"Listen, Everly, I probably shouldn't tell you this, but it's been a long fucking time for me. I want a little taste of heaven before I get inside of you. The moment I get my pants off, it's going to be fast fuck the first time."

Most women wouldn't like that kind of honesty, but

I'm definitely not like most woman. I smile. "The first time. I like the sound of that."

He leans forward and he presses my legs further apart. The cool air slides over my body as he kisses one thigh, then gives me a love bite on the other one. I jolt at the short, sharp pain. It travels to my core, causing my inner muscles to contract. Goosebumps rush over my flesh as he licks the spot he bit. He runs the flat of his tongue over the now sensitive skin.

Oh, fuck me. He's barely touch me at the this point and I'm ready to come. He has a magic mouth to go along with those magic hands.

He skims his tongue up to my pussy. Tingles follow wake of his lick. I'm embarrassingly wet. It's not that I'm a prude, the exact opposite, but the truth is this man seems to have some kind of ability to make me lose control. That I do not like. I feel helpless to stop it. Usually that's not something that I like to feel, especially in the bedroom, but with Quinn—a man I barely know—I feel safe. For once I just want to enjoy this, not worry about who has the most control and lose myself in pleasure.

Quinn dips the tongue inside of my core sending another jolt of electric need coursing through my veins. God, this man, he knows exactly how to touch me after just a few minutes. Without pulling his mouth away from my pussy, he settles my legs over his shoulders, then he slips his hands beneath my ass, his fingers digging into my flesh as he doubles his efforts. His tongue is a miracle of miracles, like I would say bronze that sucker, but then he couldn't use it on me.

I buck up against him when he takes my clit between

his teeth, my inner muscles spasming. Jesus, I'm so close, but he's not letting me fall over into the abyss of pleasure. Instead, he holds me close to the edge, pushing me closer and closer, but keeping me just out of reach of my orgasm. My toes curl as I push up hard against his mouth.

"Fuck."

I mutter the word, frustration clear in my tone. I feel his mouth curve against my skin, and I realize just how intimate this is. It's not like I haven't had oral before. I mean...I *am* the queen of one-night-stands, but there's something achingly amazing about this moment, about the way his hands move over me, the way he tastes me as if I am the most amazing treat he's ever had.

He pulls back and smiles up at me, that damned lopsided smile with the one dimple that has my nipples so hard I could probably cut a bitch with them.

"Tsk, tsk, what a dirty mouth." God, that voice, that accent. I have always been a sucker for a Texas man. They have a way of drawing out the syllables that make me so fucking wet. And his eyes are dancing and right then, I need him inside of me.

Now.

Like I know I thought it earlier, but my body might just expire if he doesn't do it in the next couple of seconds. Which is impossible since he's still dressed.

I open my mouth to order him to get naked, but he leans down again, his tongue on my clit, his fingers inside of me and he pushes me so fast over the edge I see stars. All the tension he built explodes.

"Quinn!" I cry out into the quiet hotel room as stars

explode behind my eyelids. Pleasure pulses through my entire body.

He gives me one last lick before pulling back slightly. When I look down my body at him, it's to see him licking his lips again as if he needs to have ever drop of my need inside of his mouth. He wiggles his brows and I laugh. I can't help it. I don't mind laughing with a man, but I can't remember the last time a man made me this happy.

He lets my legs fall away as he stands to his full height. He reaches behind him, tugging off his shirt. Oh, man, that a beautiful body. He's not overly sculpted but he's in shape and his big, with broad shoulders, and—surprise—a nipple ring. Then I let my gaze travel further down to where his hands are unbuttoning and unzipping his jeans. He shoves them down along with some knit boxers then steps out of them.

Oh, good god, he's beyond amazing. A thin happy trail of light hair bisects his abs and leads to the prettiest dick I've probably ever seen. He's thick, long, and curved up against his belly. There's a thick vein on the underside that I want to run the tip of my tongue along. I lick my lips.

"Absolutely not," he says and my gaze shoots to him. "I want inside you, Everly."

I open my mouth but he stops me by leaning down to kiss me. I can taste my desire on his tongue as he slips it into my mouth. I shiver in reaction. By the time he pulls back, I'm ready to do anything he wants.

After grabbing a condom out of the box, he rips open the package, then rolls it on. He does it so fast, that I blink, but I'm not complaining because I want that bad boy inside of me.

"All the way up," he says, scooping me off the bed, then tossing me lightly before I can respond. I'm laughing again. There is just something about him that makes me lighter.

Then, he's covering me, his fingers plucking my nipples, then sliding them down to my pussy. As he curls two fingers inside of me, I bow off the bed. How does he do that? He has me almost ready for another orgasm and he's barely touched me.

Before I can reach the pinnacle, he pulls his fingers out of me. Rising to his knees, he grabs my hips and enters me in one, hard thrust.

"Fuck," he grinds out. "You feel like fucking heaven."

I twine my legs around him as he starts moving inside of me. His strokes are hard and long, and every now and then he swivels his hips in just that perfect way to hit a spot deep inside me.

He leans down taking my mouth in a bruising kiss as he continues to thrust harder and harder. Every nerve ending in my body is shimmering, my need going to new heights. Quinn kisses a path down to my breasts, taking a nipple into his mouth and grazing his teeth over it before biting it gently.

That has me spiraling again, my orgasm slamming into me harder than my first one, causing me to buck up against him as he continues to ride me through my release.

Just as I am coming down, his movements increase

and after two more hard thrusts deep inside of me, he finds his release.

"Fuck, yes, Everly."

I don't know why, but hearing the way he says my name, as if I am the only person in the world, brings tears my eyes for a moment. I blink them away because of course, like I said, I don't want to freak out my one-night stand.

I expect him to fall on top of me after that performance, but he doesn't. Instead, he rolls us over so that I am on top of him, while he's still inside me. This man has all the moves.

I move to get off of him, but he holds me in place with his hands on my hips.

"Naw, stay right there for a little bit."

His voice is sleepy and filled with spent happiness. And truthfully, I would never do this because this constitutes cuddling. Definitely not in Everly Spencer's rules for her vajacations. But I can't help it. I lay back down onto of him, my head on his chest, listening to his heartbeat. I'll just take a few moments to enjoy this.

It's my last thought as I nod off to sleep.

4

HAWTHORNE BROTHER TEXT THREAD

Carter: *Quinn, please tell me you're getting some.*
Carter: *I mean, you didn't even have to work for it. I found the perfect girl for you so you owe me. I take cash, credit, and Whataburger gift cards in payment.*
Carter: *Fuck, that would make me a pimp, right?*
Carter: *I would be a baller pimp.*
Grady: *It's the middle of the fucking night. Stop texting.*
Carter: *You should be busy with Sydney. Go away.*
Grady: *JFC, I swear to God, stop texting.*
Carter: *I think crabby pants didn't get any tonight.*
Grady: *This is why Mom doesn't fucking love you.*
Carter: *Not true. I'm her favorite.*
Grady: *False. Gavin is giving her a grandbaby. Face it, guys, we all finish last after Gavin now.*
Gavin: *#favoriteson*
Carter: *#lies*
Grady: *I am muting all of you.*
Carter: *#morelies You can't not know what is going on.*
Grady: *For the love of God, it's 4 in the morning.*

Carter: *I haven't heard from Quinn so I'm worried.*
Grady: *He's a big boy. He can handle it.*
Carter: *Gavin, tell him. Quinn has a sensitive soul.*
Gavin: *I am in the same room as you, asshole. Why don't you just talk to me?*
Carter: *I could ask you the same thing.*
Gavin: *I am too old to babysit.*
Carter: *Well, then you better do something quick because having a baby means 2 am wakeup calls with screaming. And not the good kind of screaming.*
Grady: *WTAF is good screaming?*
Carter: *You know. The sex kind. *Sex-angry-sex-gif**
Gavin: *Jesus.*
Carter: *Nope. Carter.*
Carter: *But really…should we be worried? I mean, maybe he's too busy to answer the texts. Or maybe he's dead.*
Grady: *If he's dead, worrying about it isn't going to do us any good.*
Carter: **Joey-gasp-gif**
Carter: *QUINN, IF YOU ARE BEING HELD SOMEWHERE, TEXT ME!*
Gavin: *You know he isn't going to let me sleep now, right?*
Grady: *Sucks to be you. Muting y'all.*
Carter: *Fine but if he turns up dead, I'm going to tell Mom you didn't care.*
Gavin: *And I'll tell Mom you introduced him to his killer.*
Carter: *You both suck. Fucking twins. #twinsareevil*

5

QUINN

The buzzing of my phone wakes me up just before dawn. I open my eyes and realize I'm in a hotel room that I don't recognize. I didn't have much to drink last night, but it had been a long day, and the sex had worn me out.

Sex? I haven't had sex in months. Well, in about eighteen of them, but who's counting? But the entire night comes rushing back to me and I remember where I am.

Fuck.

I looked over at the sleeping form next to me.

Everly.

The night comes rushing back to me. I took her three more times after the first, and it was probably one of the best nights of my life. I have never been so in tune with a woman before in my life.

My phone starts buzzing again, so I grab it, worried it might wake up Everly.

There are a lot of texts. Seems Carter was worried about me.

Me: *I'm fine.*
Carter: *THANK THE SWEET BABY JESUS.*
Carter: *I had the cops on the phone.*
Me: *Please tell me you didn't do that.*
Carter: *Okay, I didn't do that.*
Gavin: *He did, and they told him you had to be missing seventy-two hours.*
Carter: *#lies*
Gavin: **pic of Carter talking to cops**
Carter: *Sue me. I care about you.*
Gavin: *We're heading back. Do you want us to swing by and pick you up?*

I glance over at Everly again.

If there is one woman that had been made for me, it was this one. Not in a happily ever after kind of way. I'm not some nut job who has one night of the most amazing sex ever and think it spells forever. I know that this kind of spark usually fades.

But, damn if she isn't perfect for my needs. I thought I would get my rocks off, then head out. She made it very clear that she wasn't into more than one night. When she didn't kick me to the curb last night—really early this morning—I stayed. I mean, snuggling with her was almost as good as the sex.

Nope. Don't do that. I can already feel myself getting attached. I need to be just like Carter. She knows what I wanted, she waned the same thing, and now I need to make sure that I keep it easy. No regrets and no attachments. But, I don't have to rush off.

Me: *No. I'll hire a car if I need one.*
Gavin: *Cool.*

Carter: *I want all the details. ALL OF THE DETAILS.*
Me: **absolutely-fucking-not-gif**

She stirs, her eyes blinking open. I know the moment her gaze focuses on me. She offers me a sleepy smile and stretches her arms over her head. One nipple peeks out over the covers and I can't resist brushing my fingers over it.

"Good morning," she murmurs, telling me she doesn't regret that I stayed over night with her in her room. Her voice is filled with warmth and the morning wood I woke up with goes to full staff.

"Morning," I say, setting my phone down on the beside table.

"I had fun last night."

"I know you did."

She chuckles. "Kind of full of yourself, huh?"

"I made you come at least four times. I say that's a fun time."

Her eyes dance. "I'll tell you a little secret, if you promise not to let it go to your head."

"Which one?"

Her gaze dips down then back up. A fine blush colors her cheeks and I notice that she does that whenever I give her a compliment. She comes off as a badass, but I sense there's more to her than what she shows everyone.

"Both."

"I'll try."

"Actual number of orgasms?"

I nod. She holds up her fingers indicating seven. I feel my eyes widen and it's her turn to nod.

"So, are you heading back to Texas today?"

I still think it's weird that we ran into each other but then again, I've run into old classmates from my San Antonio high school while in New York.

"No. I have about a day and a half left here."

"Got any plans?"

She shakes her head. "I was supposed to be here with my friend, but she had some family stuff to take care of."

"And you were here for work?"

She frowns at me. "We promised, no backgrounds."

Her one thing from last night. No last names. No information about our lives. Although I know she's here for work and she knows I'm here with my brothers.

"I know we have rules."

"For good reasons."

I don't roll my eyes at her but it's a close thing.

I go to reach for her but she laughs and scoots away. "Be right back."

I watch her saunter off to the bathroom and I have to admit, I like a confident woman. There is no break in her stride or even looking over her shoulder. She knows I'm looking and her completely nude body and she is okay with it. It makes her sexy as fuck.

I collapse on the mattress and sigh. It was a lot damned time between sexual partners and Carter was right. My marriage had been falling apart and the sex had been almost non existent. Worse, when we did have sex those last few months, it had been bad. And not in the good way of bad, but so bad that I could barely remember it.

I know without a doubt that I'll remember every sigh Everly uttered last night until the day I die.

The bathroom door opens and I'm sad to see she's wearing a kimono style robe that stops at mid thigh. I'd much rather she still be naked.

She's apparently beyond perceptive. "Aw, don't worry, sexy. I'll be naked soon enough."

"So, today?"

"You have nothing to do?"

I shake my head. "Sightseeing?"

"I have a better idea," she says, climbing onto the mattress and then crawling closer to me. "How about we order a decadent breakfast then work it off with another marathon of sex?"

Fuck, she's the sexiest woman I have ever known. Confidence is a turn on for me and damn, she has that in spades. And I am not a stupid man so when she kisses her way down my torso, I don't stop her and surrender to her talented hands and mouth.

She trails her tongue over my cock, then lifts it up, stroking me as she licks my balls.

Jesus.

I wasn't a virgin when I met her last night, but she has done the most amazing things to my body that I've ever experienced. It's like with her, I just let myself feel and that's a big thing for me. Like a lot of authors, I get in my head too much. She licks her way from my sac, up my shaft, all the way to the tip of my dick before taking me into her mouth.

My hands go to her head, my fingers tangling into her silky hair. Soon, it isn't enough. I need to be inside of her. Mainly because I am about to lose it in her mouth and while that is hot as fuck, I need to be deep inside her when I come again. I can't explain, never really had this need to be connected, even with my ex, which is sad, but I am not thinking about that right now. All I want now is Everly.

I tug her away from me and roll us over the mattress.

"Hey," she says, but she is also laughing at the same time. It brings me such joy to hear that. It sinks into me, lighting my soul in happiness.

I slip my hand down her body and find her hot and wet. I want to taste her, but I am close. I grab a condom off the nightstand, put it on with amazing speed with my shaking hands. I rise to my knees before pulling her hips off the bed so that I can enter her all the way to the hilt in one, hard, fast thrust.

We both moan, before I start to move. It doesn't take long to get her off—in never does. My fingers dig into her flesh as I drive harder and harder into her. Everly wraps her legs around me, pushing me into her deeper, giving me the perfect angle as I continue to fuck her sweet pussy.

"Come, Everly. Come on my dick."

She is already coming before I finish my sentence, pulling me in deeper, her muscles contracting on me. I'm thrusting so hard into her I push her over the edge once more before I finally give in. A tingle sparks down my spine as I thrust twice more, than lose it, holding her her hips off the bed, groaning her name as I pour myself into her.

I collapse on top of her a few moments later. I have no choice since I am now boneless. Everly doesn't complain.

Instead, she wraps her arms around me and tightens her legs.

Once I gain enough energy, I roll us over again so she's on top.

I sigh, trailing my fingers up and down her spine.

"So, you have nothing on your agenda today?" she asks.

"I was hoping you were going to keep using me as your sexual plaything."

She lifts up to smile down at me. Last night I thought she was hot, but in the daylight, she is beyond gorgeous. She doesn't have any makeup on, and with the hazy morning sun peeking through the curtains, she's a goddess who could easily steal my heart.

Fuck. What the hell is that. This is a fling, one night with a woman who wants just that off of me. I can't complicate things by falling for a woman who I just met. I mean, that's insane. Right?

"I agree with that idea. I just need food and a little nap."

It takes me a second to remember what I said about sex.

"Agreed."

She offers me a grin and I feel my heart tug a little. I fight against it. I will not be falling for another unavailable woman. I am just going to enjoy the time we have together and walk away.

After giving me a quick kiss, she snuggles closer, her hand over my heart. I try not to read into it, and I am not, but I can't help the way it makes me feel all warm and fuzzy inside.

I'll keep that to myself since I am pretty sure Everly wouldn't be too happy about it.

6

EVERLY

Later in the day, we find a taco stand that has high reviews and gorge ourselves on their tasty offerings.

"Other than Texas, there are only two places in the US with comparable tacos and that's Denver and LA," Quinn says.

"I would have to add San Diego in there. I haven't been to Arizona yet."

"I prefer Texas, though. I like the yellow cheese."

I smile at him, then shove another bite in my mouth. It's the easiest thing, sitting there on a bright day in Denver and eating tacos. Other guys, they would talk about what they owned and how much money they made in the last year. Quinn is definitely different. He lives in the moment and that's something I can truly appreciate.

"Yeah, I do too."

He leans forward and presses his thumb against the corner of my mouth, wiping off a bit of sour cream. He licks his thumb without taking his gaze from mine. I'm not embarrassed to admit that I almost come watching him. There is just something about him, something that clicks between the two of us. It should scare me, but it doesn't.

"So, we can't talk about too much, but we can be vague about our backgrounds, right?"

I cock my head and study him. Quinn is unassuming at first glance, but anyone who thinks there is not more going on behind those very beautiful eyes would be making a huge mistake.

"Are you a profiler?"

He snorts. "Like for the FBI?"

I nod.

"Nope."

I narrow my gaze and he laughs. "I swear. Why would you ask?"

"You seem…easy at first."

"Is this because I gave you seven orgasms our first night together?" The women sitting at the picnic table next to ours all turn in our direction.

I look at them and I realize he was trying to embarrass me. He apparently doesn't know me well enough. "He did. He's really good in bed." Then I turn back to him ignoring the way all the women are gaping at us. "It's hard to embarrass me."

"I like that about you."

"So you aren't an FBI profiler. Are you a cop?"

"Good god, no. They have to get up in the morning and wear a uniform, right?"

I smile. "Yeah, I hate mornings too."

"The worst. My whole family are early birds. And

they're happy. Like jump out of bed and take on the day with a smile. They can do all of this without coffee."

"Ugh, that's my best friend."

When he smiles, I know he got me.

"You're horrible."

He laughs out loud, throwing his head back. The sun is picking up the golden strands God, he's gorgeous.

After he finally calms down, he crosses his arms across his chest. "Not really. And I don't need names or places, but what can it hurt to talk a little bit about ourselves."

"Are you sure you aren't a cop? Do you know Jon Howard?" Jon Howard is the asshole who created an app for all the gossipy old biddies in Juniper.

"I have no idea who that is. Seriously."

I nibble on my bottom lip. It's hard for me to open up to people I know well, let alone someone I just met.

"I'll go first to show you how easy it is. I am one of four brothers."

"Jesus."

He nods. "Although, my youngest brother says the other two don't count as two since they were twins. He told my mom they were a twofer."

"Did she hit him?"

"No. My dad gave him a slap to the back of the head, and then Mom hid all the cookies."

"It's amazing he made it to adulthood."

"That was last week."

I can't help it. I snort.

"Now, it's your turn."

I don't normally give into guys trying to find out about

me. I'll be honest, it usually has me running for the hills. Quinn, though, he's different.

"I have two brothers."

"Older? Younger?"

"I'm the middle child."

"Ah, okay, we have that in common. I'm the one between the twins and younger aforementioned cookieless youngest brother."

He's charming in a way that isn't slimy. I can appreciate that after dealing with manboys in my business.

"It's the worst, right? The oldest can do nothing wrong, and the youngest is allowed to do whatever he wants."

He nods. "And I have two overachievers in my family. All three of them are truly."

"And you aren't?"

His smile fades and I instantly regret asking. This is why I don't share things. It keeps it light and all about sex.

"Never mind."

"No. It's...I have been in a rut a bit with my work. That's all. That's why I came here with my brothers. I needed a break."

I nod. "Yeah. I live in a small town and every now and then, I just have to get out of there."

A look of understanding flits over his expression. "Same. I mean, I live Sa...sorry. I live in a big city. Well, I spend part of my time in another state, both big cities. Being the only person in my family who doesn't work in the family business can be a little daunting."

"Do they resent you for not doing it?"

He shakes his head. "In fact, they're happy I found my way to do something else. I believe it was my mother who said creative types did not do well in the business. At least for what I would have been doing. She was worried it would smother me."

"She sounds like a good mom."

"What about yours?"

I sigh. I hate talking about this because it instantly ruins the mood. "She and my father died in a wreck. I was only twelve."

"Oh. Man, that must have been horrible. But before that. Do you have any good memories?"

I smile, thinking back to the things we would do. "Mom and I were kindred spirits. It was two to three against the stinky boys."

He smiles, that sweet dimple popping out. "Yeah, that's something Mom always complains about."

"And we both had the same culinary skills."

"That would be?"

"Bad. Really bad," I laugh. "But we didn't hesitate to try things. Like this souffle."

"You decided to make one of the hardest things to bake?"

She snorts. "We liked a challenge."

"What did she do?"

"She was an accountant, but mainly she handled the family business, which I thankfully didn't have to go into. But I got her head for numbers."

"And you do what with that?"

God, he is good. I think he's lying about being an agent or cop. He could definitely give any interrogator a run for his money. "I own a business with my best friend, but that is all I am going to tell you."

He holds up his hands in surrender.

"What do you do with your creativeness?"

The moment I ask, his mouth curves into a sexy smile. Dammit, I fell right into his trap, but I can't help wanting to know everything about him. Was this the plan? Lure me in with simple questions?

"I do a little drawing. A little writing."

I nod knowing that makes sense. The man is a genius with those hands. Just thinking about it sends heat spiraling through every pore. I shiver.

"Eyes up here, woman."

It's then that I realize I was staring at his hands, but it's hard not to. He has long tapered fingers that know just how to curl inside of me...I squirm on my seat.

He leans forward and lowers his voice, so only I can hear him. "If you keep staring at me like that, I'll have to have you walk in front of me." I study his expression and realize he's serious. That heat...it's a four alarm fire blazing inside of me. I nibble on my bottom lip. His gaze drops to the action and his nostrils flair. "You're killing me, Everly."

That Texas accent kills me every time he says my name. He draws out my name.

"Well, that was enough tacos. Let's go," I say, jumping up off my seat and grabbing his hand and tugging him behind me. He chuckles, but he does as I order.

"So, this is weird," I say looking at the security point. We're at Denver International Airport and I'm heading back to Texas today. I spent two nights with a guy, that's a first, but it's even odder that I'm allowing him to drop me off. I mean...I needed a ride and he had a car that was driving him back to where he was staying with his family. I know he wanted to tell me more about it, but he had stayed within the parameters.

"Yeah?" he asks, pulling me over by the bank of windows. "Why?"

"I don't normally..." I sigh. "I wasn't lying about the rules. I don't spend this much time with a guy."

And admitting it is stupid. Really stupid. Why are you letting this guy into your head, Everly?

I have no answers for my other self. She's the part of me that has kept me safe from assholes since Trent.

"Whoa, where are you at, Everly?" I blink and look at him. "Ah, that's better."

"Sorry. Just woolgathering."

He nods in understanding.

"I guess I better get going."

He frowns and looks a little bit like he's being denied a treat. "Why can't we just go back to the hotel and stay there forever?"

I chuckle. "Maybe you're independently wealthy, but I'm not."

He gets a funny look on his face, but he says nothing and it slips away before I can ask about it. "How about this?"

"What?"

"We exchange numbers."

I open my mouth to remind him that I don't do that, although the usual conviction that's there isn't. In fact, it's hard to even remember why I shouldn't want to do it. But he stops me.

"If you hate texting with me, you can block me."

"That's rude."

He chuckles. "So using me for orgasms and not knowing my last name isn't rude, but that is?"

He says it loud enough for other people to hear and an older woman gasps. I shake my head at his attempt at embarrassing me again.

"Come on, Everly. Just this little bit. Plus...I'm going to California in a few weeks. We could meet up."

That is totally off limits, something I avoid at all costs, but...he's smiling at me and when he looks at me like that, I can't tell him no.

"Tell you what. I'll give you my number, then you can decide. It's all in your hands."

I give in because I can't resist. This man does something to me, makes me yearn to be a different kind of a woman. And while I know it's a mistake, I give him my phone. He takes it, programs his number into it, then hands it back to me. I laugh out loud when I see the name he gave himself.

"Seven? Really?"

"I thought you should be reminded about what I can do for you."

I rise up on my tip toes, and kiss him. His arms wrap around my waist, pulling me against him. Sparks explode in my body, just from a sweet kiss. This is why I can't resist him. I have an active and fulfilling sex life, but with him, it's different. And maybe it's time to explore it.

"I gotta go."

He nods as he walks to the end of the line. Thanks to my TSA Precheck, I get through security fast, and wave at him before I walk down the hallway. Ugh, why do I feel like I'm going to cry? I barely know him and I feel as if I just left my best friend at the gate.

I'm early—as usual for me— so I grab a pretzel and soda. Don't judge me. It's a rule that you're supposed to have unhealthy things to eat in airports. I settle down in front of my gate and pull out my phone. Becca's been texting all morning about how irritated she is with Wyatt—nothing new there.

Becca: *I hope you still love me after I kill your brother.*

I know without asking which one it is.

Me: *Uh, what did Wyatt do now?*

Becca: *I stopped by with my brothers to have a hamburger and the new bartender asked for my number.*

Oh, yeah, I could see how Wyatt wouldn't like that. He's such a dumb ass for not asking Becca out—who is equally in love with him. Well, they are both dumb asses about it, but I know better than to stick my nose into it.

Me: *And?*

Becca: *He told him I was off limits.*

Becca: *How many times do you think he did that?*

Probably over a hundred, but I'm not going to text that.

Me: *What did your brothers do?*

Becca: *They said they agreed, so I disowned them for today.*

I roll my eyes. Becca doesn't know how to be mean to people she loves.

Becca: *Then I told Mom and she tore them new ones.*

I smile.

Me: *Good.*

Becca: *So, will you still be my best friend if I kill Wyatt.*

Me: *Oh, sweetie, I will happily help you hide the body.*

Becca: *Yay!*

Becca: *So I guess you had fun in Denver?*

Me: *Yeah.*

Becca: *Did you just not give me explicit details about the guy you hooked up with?*

I sigh. She's the best bestie in the world, but she also knows me too well. Usually I am okay with talking about the guys I sleep with, but with Quinn, I want to keep that to myself.

Thinking of his name makes me pull up his contact info.

I ignore Becca's follow up texts and try to come up with something to text him.

Me: *So...how does this work?*

I expect him not to text me back right away. I was wrong.

Seven: *However the fuck we want it to.*

My lips curve at the answer. He might not know me well, but he sure as hell understands me more than most people do after a year of being exposed to me. The idea of meeting him in California for some more fun intrigues me. It goes against my rules, but I haven't had as much fun out of bed—and I will be honest in bed—with a man in years. He was funny and affectionate. Usually, I'm okay with the first one, and not okay with the second one. I really don't know why, but something in that big lug of a man calls to me. And really, it wasn't a hard and fast rule. It was more of a guideline.

Even knowing that's a lie, knowing that this is probably a big mistake, I can't help but text him back.

Me: *Okay. So, California?*

7

QUINN

The week that follows my trip to Denver is kind of insane, but in a good way. I continue to text with Everly every day. I didn't expect it from her. I hoped, but I definitely knew she has intimacy issues. Still, she keeps texting me.

Work is rocking and moving right along. I spent three days holed up in my house, ignoring texts from my brothers just to get done with this new idea I had. Now, I stare at the character I created and realized I just drew Everly.

Shit. It *is* her. I blink at the drawing and I just can't think straight. Did I know that I was doing it? Maybe. There is no doubting it's her. Those big brown eyes that look deceptively innocent until you saw the smirk and her amazing body.

Fuck.

I've never really drawn anyone in my personal life. People know that Danvers is sort of based on me. He looks like me, there is no doubt about that. Granted, I would never make it as a cop in the present or future. I get to live out my fantasies this way, all the while enjoying air conditioning and sleeping until at least ten in the morning. Still, I have never included other real people in my books. I think it always bothered Abby that I didn't draw her into the series. Granted, I drew her constantly, but she wanted the notoriety of being in one of my books. We really were not compatible, I think with a shake of my head.

If someone Everly knows reads this book, they'll know it's her. Especially since I wrote her damned name beneath the drawing. That means I have already named her in my head and there will be no changing it, unless my editor hates it, which she won't. She's been bugging me telling me I need more women in the books, so this apparently is my way of moving into that. I pick a woman I can't stop thinking about and won't give me her last name.

Was I in a trance?

Maybe. That's the way I've felt since I met Everly. Not even during my teen years did I spend days fantasizing about a woman. I mean, okay, I might have fantasized a little too much about Destiny's Child back in the day, but not truly about most girls I knew in person. I was too interested in my art to notice any of the stuck up snobs I went to school with. They always were trying to get Grady's attention or turn Gavin who came out when he was ten.

But with Everly, I can't get her out of my head. I even dream about her.

As if on cue, my phone buzzes.

Everly: *There are times I wish I was an only child.*

I smile. She might not give me names and she might think she is keeping things from me, but she tells me more than she knows.

Me: *What did they do now?*

Everly: *Idiot #1 is a stubborn asshole.*

Me: *What did he do?*

Everly: *Nothing. Just a statement on his personality.*

Me: *And #2?*

Everly: *He's hiding in my house because one of the LOLs is trying to set him up with her granddaughter.*

Everly: *And granted, I agree with him. The woman is a viper and would eat him alive, not in a good way.*

I laugh.

Me: *Why don't you go out then?*

Everly: *It's too peopley out there. I hate tourists.*

God, I feel like I should know where she lives. She's given me enough clues, and there is something familiar about the LOLs, but I don't know where I've heard of them before.

Everly: *So how are things with you, Seven?*

Everly: *Is it weird that your nickname is the same as a serial killer movie?*

Me: **seven-brad-pitt-whats-in-the-fucking-box-box-pissed-gif**

Everly: *God I love that movie.*

Me: *We should watch it together.*

Everly: *When we go to CA?*

Me: *No. Tonight.*

The moment I send the message, I realize I'm pushing

her too much. She wants her distance and for the time being, I am okay with that. I'm not sure I want more, but there is something about this woman who tugs at me. From the moment I saw her, touched her, tasted her...

Fuck. I'm hard, again.

Everly: *Like we watch it at the same time and text?*

Not really, but I feel that might be the best thing I can get right now. She's skittish and if I push her too fast, she might just disappear on me.

Me: *Yeah.*

There's pounding on my door and I toss a frown at it. I don't want to deal with anyone. Not when I almost have her talked into watching a movie with me.

And yes, I know it's probably pathetic, but I miss her.

"Open up, Quinny."

I hate when Carter calls me that. When he was really young, like preschool age, I let him call me that. Now, it just annoys me, which is why he does it. Asshole.

The three little dots are bouncing telling me that she is writing me back. I slip my phone into my pocket—Carter would be too nosey—and I go to the door.

When he sees me, his eyes widen. "Whoah, you look like a mountain man, Quinn."

"Is that why you're here? To tell me I look like a mountain man?"

"No. I thought I would get you out of the house..." he takes a step closer then blinks. "Jesus, when was that last time you bathed."

"Yesterday." Lies. It was three days ago. Okay, maybe four. "I've been working."

He eyes me skeptically.

"Really. I have. That trip we took to Denver seems to have cleaned out the cobwebs in my brain."

He smiles. "Those aren't the cobwebs that got cleaned out."

He will been insufferable if I let him in on the fact that she's the reason I am jamming again. My phone vibrates in my pocket, and I almost reach for it.

"So, I don't want to go out."

"Really? Don't you want to celebrate?"

"No. I've been up forty-eight hours, so I need a shower, a meal and bed. I'll take a raincheck though."

"Good. I will hold you to it."

He will, but hopefully not soon.

Once the door is shut behind him, I pull out my phone and there are three texts from Everly.

Everly: *I might be up for that.*

Everly: *What time?*

Everly: *Also, should we be naked for this?*

I roll my eyes as my dick throbs. This woman is going to be the death of me.

Me: *How about eight?*

Me: *And I hope if we do it naked, I get pics.*

And again, I instantly regret sending it. Jeez, what a creepy as fuck thing to send to a woman. If I had a sister, I would tell her to block the bastard who just sent that to her. As usual, Everly shows me she is anything but the typical woman.

Everly: *Only if there is tit for tat.*

Everly: *Literally.*

My entire body is buzzing and I can't control it. Don't want to. I know it's a mistake to get this involved with a woman who won't even tell me her last name. I hit the call button before I can stop myself.

She picks up on the first ring.

"Why are you calling me?"

"I love your voice."

"Is that a fact?"

Her accent deepens when she's aroused. It sings through my entire body, heating my blood and leaving me more than a little light-headed.

"Yeah. I do."

"Who is that?" I hear some guy say in the background.

In a split second, jealousy replaces the arousal.

"None of your business, idiot. Go back into the living room."

She has a man in her bedroom? What. The. Fuck.

"I'm bored."

"Then grow a set and leave my house. Why don't you go bug Wyatt?"

Then I remember she said her brother was at her house.

"She will just sent Rhonda over there."

"Oh, no, a woman. Wait. Shouldn't you be at work?"

He mumbles something I can't make out.

"Oh, for the love of the baby Jesus and all his friends, hide in the kitchen."

"You're not a good sister."

"Never claimed to be."

I smile at her answer.

"Fine."

Then I hear him clomping away.

"Finally. God, he is a whiney baby," she says.

"I heard that!"

"Oh, eat a bag of dicks."

Then I hear a door shut.

"See what I've been putting up with?"

I chuckle. "I just got invaded by Carter."

"The pimp is there?"

"I told you to not call him that because he would like it too much."

"It is what he is." I can hear the shrug in her voice.

"And no, he isn't here. He wanted me to go out tonight."

"Oh." Was that disappointment I heard in her voice? Would she rather I go out with Carter and leave her alone. "Why not?"

"First of all, I haven't bathed in...let's just say awhile. And I'm not in the mood. I rarely am."

"Back it up, babe." Yeah, she calls me that every now and then and I can't fight the thrill that runs through me when she does. I know it's a word she probably uses for a lot of people, but I don't think about that. Mostly. "How long has it been since you took a shower and why have you not been showering?"

"Work. I just...the last forty-eight hours have been amazing and I haven't slept other than a nap here and there."

"Oh?"

She wants to know, but she's trying her best not to

ask. I hear it there in her voice, in the way she lilts it at the end of the word. I will break down her defenses.

"Yeah. But, since you won't let me come to you and take you out for a proper date, how about we have a date tonight over the phone?"

"What the hell is a proper date and why would we want to be proper?"

"Right, forgot who I was talking to. Still, you won't let me take you out on a date—"

"I don't date."

Don't I know it. She's reminded me at least once a day.

"We can date over the phone."

She doesn't say anything for a long minute. One thing I learned in Denver and since is just give her space.

"Okay."

I feel as if I won the Nobel prize just to get her to agree to a date on the phone.

"I need to shower, as I said, and I need to eat. How about I call you back in about an hour, so we can watch some good bloody murder?"

"That sounds fantastic."

"You're an interesting woman, Everly."

"You don't know the half of it."

"I'll call you back in a little bit."

"Bye."

We hang up and instantly I want to call her back. Like I said, she's the drug I need, the connection I always want. One week and I can't remember what it was like to have her in my life. Sadly, she isn't in my life, not really.

If I can reel her in, let her know that I am not a threat

to her independence, I might just get her to tell me her last name. Sad? Yes. Do I care? Nope, not if I get her last name.

With that thought, I hurry to get cleaned up and ready for our movie night "date."

8

EVERLY

As I sit in my hotel room waiting on Quinn, I wonder just what the hell I am doing in California.

I mean, I know that I got on a plane and all that crap. I bought the ticket; although, I did buy one that allowed me to change the date. Even with that, I didn't. I pulled up the site every few days and looked at the cancellation page. Then, I would remember what it felt to feel connected to him, to have him thrust deep inside of me.

With that thought, I have to fight the need to touch myself. This is just not something I do. Not really. Okay, never. I don't fly across the country to meet up with one particular man. I'm the queen of vajacations. I don't moon over a man, dream about him, get off to him and *only* to him with my trusty vibrator Sam. As many times as I've come thinking about Quinn, I probably should rename my vibrator. Does everyone have a name for their vibrator?

What was I talking about before vibrators?

Oh, yeah, Quinn.

I smile. The man is so amazing in and out of bed. I mean, don't get me wrong, I'm here to get a bit more of that big man. Those hands, that mouth, his amazing smile. God, I melt every time I see it. Hell, just thinking about it right now has me melting.

As if conjured up by my thoughts, there's a knock at the door. My heartbeat speeds up as I jump off the bed and hurry to the door. I know. Completely un-Everly-like. But I can't help it.

I look out the peephole and see him standing there. Even in the weird fisheye view, he looks like the best thing in the world. After unlocking the door, I pull it open. The moment he sees me, his eyes darken, and that mouth—you know the one that I said was amazing—kicks up on one side showing me his cute dimple.

For a second, we stand there looking at each other like complete dorks, but I can't help it. He's beautiful.

Then, he's striding into the room, tossing his duffle bag to the side as he wraps his arms around me pulling me against his body. While keeping hold of me, he grabs the do not disturb sign, slipping it on the doorknob, then letting it slam.

Before I can say anything, his mouth is on mine and god, I'm dissolving. Just right there, I can't seem to think of anything else other than falling into him, losing myself. Heat explodes inside of me as I wrap my legs around him. I press against him, gyrating my hips. He tears his mouth away from mine to groan.

"Fuck. I told myself I would take it slow when I got here."

I blink at him. "Why would you do that? We have less than thirty-six hours to spend together."

His gaze collides with mine and, again, I feel myself dissolving into a big pile of lust. I mean, you would too if you could be right where I am. When he looks at me like this, like I'm the most important thing in the world to him, it scares me. Then, his mouth curves and, Jesus, I lose any doubts I had.

"You always have the best answers," he says, his Texan accent rolling over the syllables in a lazy way that reminds me of his voice right after he wakes up.

I miss hearing it every morning I'm not with him.

And before I can panic, his mouth is on mine. I'm still clinging to him like a koala bear as he walks over to the bed. He turns so that his back is to the mattress and goes into a freefall. We land together and my mouth is on his. We are both desperate for each other. And yes, if I thought about it, I would definitely take note about how out of character this is for me, but once I get his shirt off of him and my hands trail over his pectoral muscles, I can't think of anything else but this man.

I slip my hands over his heated flesh and sigh. As the days went by, my need for him grew. It was as if I would die if I couldn't touch him again. I trail down his body, then slip from his lap onto the floor. I waste no time undoing his jeans and getting my hands on his pretty cock.

I pump him, enjoying the feel of him against my palm, and smile when a little precum leaks out. I rise up to my knees and lick it off the tip. The salty sweetness of his cum rolls through me. My entire body tingles with anticipation, my panties are damp, and my nipples are hard. I swirl my tongue around the head of his dick.

"Fuck me, Everly."

"I'm trying."

He chuckles, but it ends on a groan as I take him in my mouth. I only get him in there for a few moments before he's pulling me up to my feet and onto the bed. He tears off my clothes. Well, he gets my clothes off, but my panties are in shreds. I don't care that they cost a pretty penny. All I want is him inside of me.

Need surges as he grabs a condom and rolls it on. Then, he's rolling us over so that I'm on top of him. He slips two fingers inside of me and we both groan.

"Such a needy pussy," he says as he removes his fingers and replaces them with his thick cock

"Oh, fuck," I mutter. I feel my need grow with each inch he presses inside of me.

Once he's completely seated inside of me, he leans up, taking one of my nipples into his mouth. When I feel the scrape of his teeth against the tip, I gyrate my hips just a little. He groans against my flesh. Tiny little vibrations dance off my skin and I decide this has gone on long enough. I ease him back on the mattress and start riding him.

Soon, we are moving in rhythm together as if we were made for each other. I had wondered just how it would be this second time together, but it seems that it's even better.

"Come for me, Everly," he says, flicking his finger against my clit. It takes another flick, then a press of his fingers and I'm hurtling over the summit. My orgasm rips a scream from my throat as I convulse.

Quinn takes over. His hands are on my hips, digging into my skin as he thrusts up into me, over and over. Each time he enters me, he seems to go deeper and deeper.

"Come for me, Quinn," I say, repeating his phrase on purpose. His green gaze connects with mine. I watch as his orgasms hits. His eyes roll back in his head as he thrusts up into me one last time, holding himself there as he comes. Most men look insane when they come, but of course, not Quinn. He looks like a fucking sex god.

Then, his hand slips between my legs, pressing my clit one more time. The orgasm takes me by surprise as he swivels his hips beneath me. I gasp at the intensity of it.

Long moments later, I collapse on top of him. He wraps his arms around me as I tuck my head under his chin. I should get up, and I should be getting him out of my system, but right now, I just want to stay like this.

I WAKE UP SOME TIME LATER AND REACH FOR HIM AND FIND the bed empty but still warm. When I gain my wits, I sit up and look around the room. The curtains are open, and I see him sitting on the balcony. I got us a room with an ocean view, and I can tell from the orangey glow, the sun is setting. The door is open. I can smell the ocean in the air.

Pulling up my legs, I wrap my arms around them and watch him. Every time I see him, get a text from him...any interaction with him has me yearning for more. That hasn't happened to me in a really long time. I don't know what to do about it. This weekend was all about getting him out of my system, but I don't know if that is going to happen. Ever.

Panic has my throat closing, so I close my eyes and count backwards from ten. When I open my eyes, I realize that I am losing myself in this guy and I need to create some space. After this weekend, I will make sure that I think more about our relationship.

Oh, fuck. We don't have a relationship. We're just hooking up.

"I can hear you thinking in there."

Ugh. And there's that. Not only does the man know exactly how to get me off, but he also knows how to handle me out of bed. My offish attitude usually makes men clingy. Not Quinn. Not really. He just floats along, agreeing to my terms, and giving me massive amounts of orgasms. Why mess with a good thing?

I slip out of bed and grab the t-shirt he was wearing, slipping it over my head before I join him on the balcony. It's then that I notice he's drawing on a big pad. I don't know what he does for a living—we have stuck to that rule at least—but I know he's artistic. He's mentioned working on a project and drawing, but when my gaze lands on his work, I blink.

First of all, it's a drawing of me, asleep in bed. Second thing? It's fucking amazing.

"Wow." It's a simple word for what he's drawn. Worse, I can feel a lump rising in my throat, but this has nothing to do with panic. There's something familiar about it too.

"Thank you," he murmurs as he sets the pad on the table and takes my hand, tugging me closer and then onto his lap. He brushes his mouth over mine before sitting back.

"I knew you were artistic in some way, but that's amazing."

I'm looking at the drawing again and my stomach is now tensing. Not in a way that is actually bad, but... damn, I have no idea what's happening. Then it hits me. I look soft, approachable. No one, not even my bestie, would say that about me.

"Is that how you see me?"

"In that moment. Yeah."

"I look..." I swallow trying to come up with the words to describe it. My face is relaxed and somehow, he has added an aura of serenity around me.

"What?"

I jerk a shoulder, afraid of saying more and embarrassing myself. It's in that moment that I realize he has rendered me speechless. That is something I am just not familiar with. I mean, it happens, but normally when one of my jerk brothers says something that angers me to the point of wanting to murder them. So...every day.

This is different. His sketch has a lump forming in my throat.

"Everly?"

His tone is soft, but there is a thread of worry in it that makes me feel even worse. This is supposed to be fun. I shake my head, pushing away those worries, that vulnerability I keep away from others. Well, everyone but Becca.

He's a fling, not a man who wants feelings to invade the weekend of fun.

"It's just different."

He looks at me with an expression that tells me he knows I'm lying. "You know, we all have different sides. There are no one dimensional people. Even an evil person has a flip side."

That line sounds like a famous quote, but I can't place where I've heard it before. "I guess you're right. I'm just not..."

My voice trails off as my brain melts. It's his fault. He's looking at me as if I am the most precious thing in the world, when we both know I am the furthest thing from it.

I steel myself against all the warm butterflies taking flight in my stomach. This man. He is going to make me lose all my armor and that is not acceptable.

"So, how about we decide on dinner?"

He studies me and for a brief moment, I realize that he knows I am trying to avoid the discussion of why it bothers me. As usual, he reads me well and lets it go.

"There's a place I love to eat here that has the best tacos."

"Sold."

He leans forward and brushes his mouth against mine. Before I'm ready, he ends the kiss then sets me on my feet.

"Then get dressed, woman. I need sustenance to keep up with you."

His light tone puts me at ease. I chuckle as I hurry back in the room to get dressed. Fun and relaxation is what this weekend is all about. I intend to grab onto it with both hands and live in this amazing moment.

WE'RE AT ANOTHER AIRPORT WITH HIM SENDING ME OFF. The fact that he did it not once but twice is a little alarming, but I shove that worry to the back of my head.

"You know we're meeting up again."

Not a question, but a statement. He's feeling pretty cocky after this weekend and why not. He got me to come all the way across the country to meet up with him. And he knows it.

I sigh. "Maybe."

He gives me that one dimple smile and I know I am going to lose the fight. What is it about this man? There have been a lot who have tried, but this one, he's under my skin and crawling into my heart. That is a dangerous thing.

We reach the security check. His flight is later and at some other airport. I'm not sure what airport, but I don't question him. If I do, he will know it was killing me to know.

"Can you call me when you get home?"

I make a face.

"Text then? Just so I know you made it home safe."

I nod, giving in to him because I know I will. I rise up to my toes and brush my mouth over his, but his hands go to my hips, holding me still. Then he deepens the kiss, his tongue slipping into my mouth.

All of a sudden, an emotion I can't figure out hits me.

Tears burn the backs of my eyes. When he pulls back, we're both breathing heavily.

"Have a safe trip, Everly."

I nod, unable to speak before practically running to the pre-check station. Once I get through, I see him standing there, watching me, his hooded gaze telling me he still wants me as much as I want him.

I wave at him—a totally dorky thing to do—but when he smiles at me, I can't help the way my heart turns over. He's dangerous, but at the moment, I have control of my emotions.

And if I repeat that enough, I might believe it.

9

QUINN

"You look well rested," my mother says to me as she kisses my cheek. We're at Alamo Cafe to celebrate Syd's—Grady's one-time executive assistant and now girlfriend—promotion. I've been back in town for less than ninety minutes but thankfully, we are at the one right down 281 from the airport. I got here before everyone else.

The entire family is here, including Ollie, Gavin's husband. He splits his time between New York and Texas, so we don't get to see him as much.

"I still don't understand why you're with him," Carter says, being the regular asshole that he always is.

I might be a tad bit irritated with everything at the moment. I haven't heard from Everly. I know that her small town doesn't have an airport and she had like a two-hour drive back home, but she left thirty minutes before me.

As if conjured up by my thoughts, my phone buzzes in my pocket. I pull it out, as stealthy as I can because my mom has a no phone rule at the dinner table, no matter where we are.

Everly: *Made it home.*

Quinn: *Thank you.*

Everly: *For going home?*

Quinn: *No. For telling me you got there. I know you don't like any kind of checking in.*

Everly: *Stop that.*

Quinn: *What?*

Everly: *Jesus. Just stop trying to figure me out.*

Quinn: *I'm not doing that. Just enjoying the ride.*

Everly: *Well, I definitely did this weekend.*

Everly: *You're blushing, aren't you?*

Of course, I am. I mean, I'm in my thirties but she just knows how to tease me. Normally, I would hate it, but with Everly, I actually look forward to it.

Quinn: *No comment.*

Everly: **Joel-McHale-laughing-and-pointing gif**

Quinn: *Not funny. I'm sitting at dinner with my family.*

Everly: **pic-Everly-in-bed**

Quinn: *Are you naked?! And why are you doing this to me?*

Everly: *#sorrynotsorry*

Quinn: *Got anymore?*

Everly: *I definitely do, but I would rather show you in person.*

Quinn: *I agree with that...but still.*

Everly: *I have no naked pics, but I can send you what I would like to do to your body.*

"Quinn Matthew Hawthorne."

I look up from my phone, my ears going hot as I take in the looks I'm getting from my family.

Quinn: *Oh, shit, Mom just yelled at me about the phone.*

Everly: *#mamasboy*

Quinn: *#truestory*

"Sorry," I mumble and shove my phone in the pocket of my jeans.

"You know my rule."

Yeah, Mom has a rule about phones. Before my dad retired, he was a bit of a workaholic. Now that Grady runs the company, he's gotten a bit like our dad. All my brothers are. Gavin is a lawyer who divides his time between San Antonio and New York, and Carter seems to work 24/7. So, no phones at dinner.

"It's okay," Carter says sipping at his margarita. "He's got a romantic gal pal."

I'm going to kill him. I've had to research different ways to kill a person because of my writing, and I can say that I have no idea what happened to him. Lots of deserted country in Texas, especially as you head out of San Antonio to El Paso.

"Gal pal?" my father asks, as he leans back in his chair and drapes his arm behind my mother. They have always been a solid couple, one that makes other couples jealous.

"I think you might need to get Carter into a program." I lean closer to whisper. "He's been hearing voices again."

"So, who is this woman?" my mother asks in a tone she thinks is nonchalant. It isn't, just in case you were wondering.

"No woman."

"Then why did you go to San Diego this weekend?" Carter, the soon to be dead brother, says.

"Research."

From the look on my mother's face, I can tell she doesn't believe me. Ellen Hawthorne is no dummy. She helped my father build the At Home Network, and Dad has always said he would never have gotten it off the ground without her.

"For the new book?"

I nod. "It's going in another direction than I thought it would."

"Oh?"

I nod as the idea I've been thinking about the last few weeks starts to grow. "I'm thinking Danvers needs a partner. Change things up a bit."

"Please tell me he's finally going to get himself a woman. There's no reason your hero needs to be celibate."

I roll my eyes and share a look with Oliver. He's married to my brother, but he's been my agent longer. Let me tell you, authors love when people tell us how to write our books. LOVE IT. Especially coming from someone who hasn't read the series.

"He's not celibate. Just assholes think he is."

"Still, he needs to clean out his house."

And yes, my brother talks like that in front of my mother and Syd. I reach out with my leg and kick him in the shin.

"Ow, what the hell man?"

"Carter, I think your brother would rather not listen to you prattle on about something you know nothing about," Syd says, throwing me an understanding glance. She might have just gotten that promotion, but she worked as Dad's executive assistant first, then Grady's. Dealing with Carter was part of the job.

"I know a lot about sex."

Seriously, my brother has a death wish.

"Carter, settle down. And please, don't be so disrespectful," my mother says.

He nods, but he directs his narrowed gaze in my direction. He is definitely going to make me pay for the bruises that are forming on his shins. Don't care. It was worth it to get him to shut the hell up.

Thankfully, the food gets delivered and talk moves to Syd's new job and the romance that is now common knowledge. Seriously, we never thought Grady would get over himself and admit his feelings for her. And a month ago, I probably would have been jealous. But now, there's Everly.

Just thinking her name has my hands itching to drop my fajita and check my messages. Even when I met my ex, I wasn't this infatuated, but there is something about being with Everly. Freeing. I fight the need, push it aside because I can obsess on it later, and concentrate on my family now. It's like I'm an addict and she's the only drug I need to ease my need. I know it's insane, especially since I've spent less than a total of five days with her.

I push aside my worries and dig into my food. An hour later, my stomach is full of the best tasting fajitas and I'm feeling mellow.

"You know you don't have to hide that you have a sex life, Quinn," my mother says. Yeah, she's one of those moms. She showed me how to put a condom on using a cucumber when I was fifteen. I don't know if she was trying to teach me or make sure I didn't have sex because that's an image not helpful to a guy.

"I know."

"I'm just happy that you're getting out there. You've seemed happier these last few weeks."

"I have?"

She nods. "You seemed to be in a rut for the last year or so."

"I'm feeling better, mostly due to the story going so well. Although, I didn't expect the story to go this way."

"That's life though."

"I was talking about my book."

She offers me a smile. "I know, but you write Danvers' life, right? Maybe you've been stuck because you knew he needed a change. It's good to shake things up a little."

"Maybe."

"You know that I don't like to butt into your life, and I won't start now. Just know that your marriage wasn't a failure. It was just that you two weren't made for each other, and it took you awhile before you both realized it."

"That's one way to look at it."

"Oh, Quinn," she says cupping my face. "You're an author. You know there are millions of ways to look at any relationship, romantic or not."

She kisses me on the cheek and follows my father to their car. Oliver is next to step up and start in on me. Seriously, my family.

His dark brown eyes narrow as they study my face. He's trying to look like a badass, and yes, he is one, but I know he has a soft spot for his favorite brother-in-law. "So, a new direction you forgot to tell your agent about?"

"Sorry. Still working on the ideas, but the pictures are flowing. You know what that means."

"That you're on to something good." He nods. "Good. You've needed to shake things up a bit."

I'm getting sick of people saying that to me. It makes me think they got together to work out a possible intervention. "And you waited until now to tell me?"

He shrugs. "Don't fuck with the genius."

I feel my mouth twitch because that is his motto with all of his clients. He might be a little dramatic himself, but I think that's why he knows how to deal with artistic types.

"And I know that there is no reason for you to research a place you have been to a billion times thanks to Comic-Con, but I'll let it go. Got a date for me?"

I think about what I have and what I need to clean up in the story. "Give me about eight weeks."

He nods as Gavin walks up and they walk off together, hand in hand. Sydney and Grady have hurried off already. Carter, unfortunately, is still here.

"So, how about we go check out some clubs tonight?"

Again, this is work for him and while I know he's very good at it, I'm not in the mood for him. Or his bullshit after what he pulled earlier. I just take off to my car. When I reach it, I realize he's parked next to me. Of course.

"Come on, stop being mad at me."

I say nothing as I punch the button to unlock the doors.

"I'm sorry."

I blink and look over at him. Carter hardly ever apologizes. "Thanks."

"Even though you know I'm right, and I was the one who got you the hook up."

"I went to San Diego for research."

He snorts. "You don't have to lie to me. I know you went there to meet with her."

I look up at the wide expanse of stars across the sky. "Why me?"

"Cuz I love you best. I'm just glad you have found someone." Then he pauses. "No club tonight?"

"Why?"

"There's this little club that's garnering attention on weeknights."

See. He might be a goofball, but his mind is always on work. "Not dressed for it."

"Do you even have a suit? Wait, you do have one, right?"

"Oh, so you're playing the asshole in this scenario? I think I'll head home."

"Sorry. And it doesn't matter. Tonight is their country night or something like that."

"Okay. But only until midnight."

"Yay! Let's park at your house and you can drive."

"Why?"

"You won't drink." And Carter doesn't either, but I decide not to point that out. This way, I can just leave him when I feel like it.

As I slip into my car, I pull out my phone to check my texts.

Everly: *So, dinner with the folks, huh? My BFF and I are having margaritas for dinner.*

That is the most information she has given me about her life. I'm like a junkie who is jonesing for another hit.

Everly: *Okay, never mind. That was a bad idea. Now we are just going to have big burgers and fries.*

Everly: *I know that you are sad you are missing this conversation.*

I smile down at the phone.

Me: *I am, actually. Instead, I got accosted about my personal life at dinner.*

Everly: *By your parents?*

Me: *More like my brother Carter.*

Everly: *The pimp?*

I laugh out loud, just before there's a knock on the window. Carter is standing there, an exaggerated frown on his face. Before I can stop him, he opens the door.

"You said you would go."

"Sorry. Just had some...emails."

He rolls his eyes and tries to grab my phone.

"Hey, asshole. I won't go if you don't take a step back."

"I saw my name on the screen. You're texting with Everly."

"I said you were being a dick at dinner, and she mentioned you were my pimp."

"Hot damn," he says, clapping. "I like it. Carter Hawthorne, Pimp at Large. Let's go. I only have you for a few hours."

I nod as he hurries over to my passenger door.

"Hey, what the hell are you doing?"

"I talked to the manager and asked if it was okay to

leave my car here. He said it was okay as long as I pick it up by noon."

"Let's get this show on the road."

Knowing that it is better to do exactly that so I can get home at a reasonable hour, I do as he says.

10

EVERLY

The sound of deranged quacking is the first thing that wakes me up the week after another trip to meet up with Quinn. Murderous rage pours through me. I'm going to kill those freaking ducks.

I bolt out of bed to go yell at the mallards that show up for breakfast every morning, but my stomach rolls over. It's the second day in a row this has happened, so I know what's coming, so I rush to the bathroom.

I am tossing what was an excellent meal at my brother's restaurant, The Mason Jar. I start thinking about which petri dish gave me this bout with stomach flu.

It isn't uncommon for Becca and me to have our illness schedule run hand in hand with all the kids in Juniper. They are about seventy-five percent of our clientele, so it makes sense.

I sit back on the cold floor and lean against the bathroom wall. Assholes, every one of those suckers. If they didn't clothe and feed me, I might just bar them from our shop.

It takes me a few minutes to get up off the floor and clean up. Once I brush my teeth and wash my face, I start to feel better. I've been feeling off for the last week, and it has nothing to do with ghosting Quinn.

I sigh as I press the button of my coffee maker so it can start up. A glance out the front window tells me the ducks that go from house to house for bread have moved on to Mrs. Stephenson across the street, so I go back to the kitchen.

The two male mallards showed up around a year or so ago. The couple are inseparable, so we've started calling them Bert and Ernie. We thought that maybe they were just hanging out waiting to find mates. That was until a female showed up and they both chased her off. They waddle around town, showing up in the morning for their bread and will not leave until you come out and toss some out there

I sigh and lean against the counter, trying to get my body under control. Usually, I can fight off the worst of anything that comes along, but this bug is hitting me extra hard. I'm drained at the end of the day, unable to do much else other than come home and go to bed.

Or am I depressed? It might be that. It's been over twenty-four hours since I responded to Quinn. When I left him in Ft Worth a couple days ago, I made a decision to cut him off. I needed to make a break, or he was going to ruin me. I thought I would feel better, but I don't. He keeps sending me texts. I still feel shitty for doing it, and I am not all that positive it's going to stick. He's kind of addictive.

I close my eyes the moment the room starts to spin.

I've had issues with anemia in the past and, apparently, it's back just in time to complicate the stomach bug I picked up. That leaves me unsteady on my feet. It has absolutely nothing to do with Quinn.

Except…I've started to yearn for him. Every day that goes by, it gets worse.

What insanity is that? I think about him constantly. That fact tells me it's time to step away.

I don't want to. What I want is to call him and hear his voice. I know just listening to him talk would make me feel better. But I can't because that would be leading him on, and I don't do that. I can't have attachments. It's just not in my makeup. And I know what you're about to say.

Bitch, everyone has at least one bad relationship in their past.

Yeah, I know. Believe me. I already had issues with intimacy before Trent the Asshole used me for the frat contest. Losing my parents at twelve had taught me what loss was like before I should have had to learn about those things. Juniper does march to its own drummer, but it is still a small town. Weird girls with personality disorders are not at the top of anyone's list for dates. Well, other than Josh the current sheriff and the guy who has dated almost everyone.

But I digress. So, I had limited dating experience. I was prime material for Trent the Asshole.

My phone buzzes on the counter and, of course, it's Becca.

Becca: *Hey, sunshine, how are you feeling this morning?*
Me: *Fine.*
Becca: *You can take another day off if you need to. You*

know that Wednesdays tend to be slow this time of year.

Me: *No. I think I need to get out of the house. Besides, I can just work in the backroom and take it easy.*

Becca: *Any more dizzy spells?*

Me: *No.*

Okay, and this is where you know I'm kind of an asshole. I'm not being completely honest with Becca but it's for her benefit. She's a worrier and it's nothing really. Just a combination of whatever disease the petri dishes gave me and my anemia coming back.

Becca: *I'm picking you up.*

Me: *I can drive.*

Becca: *That's debatable.*

Me: *And everyone thinks you're the sweet one.*

Becca: *I've told you that's so I can lure our victims in with my sweetness while you mix the poison.*

Becca: *Be there in about fifteen minutes.*

Me: *Fifteen minutes?!*

Becca: *I have donuts from Sugar High.*

Me: *Okay, you definitely are my best friend.*

Becca: **Jon Stewart middle finger GIF**

I don't hurry to dress. From the moment we met in grade school, we were the best of friends. Night and day, most people think. But I always say that I'm not all dark, and while Becca seems happy a lot, there's a good amount of darkness dancing around the edges. We have seen each other in various stages of undress, so I see no reason to change out of my t-shirt and boxers.

Fourteen minutes later, she lets herself into my house.

"Hey, there," she says, looking me over. "You look pale."

Ugh, Becca is the most observant, and she's not afraid of me like other people.

"I think my anemia is back."

"Everly," she says, setting down the bag of donuts on the table. "You need to see a doctor."

"I will. In fact, I was thinking of calling that new female doctor they added to the clinic."

Normally, I go to San Antonio or Austin for my appointments. Mainly because the main OBGYN in Juniper had been older than God. Also, he told me to keep my knees together instead of getting on birth control. I was eighteen and my feet were still in the stirrups, so it was beyond awkward. From that point on, I drove out of town for my yearly appointments.

"Oh, Dr. Abernathy? She's good from what I hear."

Of course, she knows about her. People in this town tell Becca everything.

"Well, that's settled. When we get to work, I'll call."

We both sit down and start in on our donuts. For someone who was just singing love songs to the porcelain god, I'm ravenous. Every bite seems better than the last.

"If you don't make an appointment, I will say something to Wyatt."

Wyatt is my older brother, who raised me. He kind of freaks out about anything to do with me or Mason, our youngest sibling. One word from Becca and Wyatt will be up in all of my business.

"Or worse. I'll tell Mama."

I frown at her. Millie Gold is the sweetest woman, but just like her daughter, she's fiercely protective and will kick my ass if she found out how sick I've been.

"No reason to threaten me. I'll do it. I want to establish care anyways. It won't take long for her to get filled up with women from this town."

"Right."

I sigh as I sip my coffee, happy that my stomach seems to be settling down. "So, you said something about your friend coming into town?"

"He said he might pop up."

"As in a date?"

She shakes her head. "No. We don't date, just friends."

"You should though."

"We tried."

"You did. When?"

She munches on her unicorn sprinkle donut—ugh—and thinks about it. "Right after you got back from meeting up with MDD."

MDD is what she calls Quinn. She has no idea what his name is because I refuse to acknowledge that I have seen him more than once. So, she started calling him Mysterious Denver Dude.

"Quit calling him that."

When I see her smile, I realize that I fell for her trickery. As I said, people think Becca's sweet as can be, but she's crafty.

"The fact that you finally acknowledged him is enough for me." She doesn't even try to hide the smugness in her voice.

"I did not—never mind. We aren't arguing about this."

"Again."

We eat in silence for a while, and I know exactly

what she's doing. She's trying to outwait me and then hope that I will spill all my secrets. I am totally not doing that.

"I didn't say it was him."

She says nothing and hums as she eats.

"Becca Magnolia Gold."

"Ohh, you three named me. Definitely upset over something."

I frown at her, but her smile softens.

"Would it be so bad to fall for a guy?"

There goes my stomach again. "You know how I feel about that."

"I do, but I think it's stupid."

"Becca."

"Listen, I get that you don't trust people to stick around. Losing your parents, well that sucked all the balls. But, seriously, because one asshole in college treated you like crap—and I'm so not downplaying what happened with Trent—doesn't mean that you can't have a relationship now."

I know it's stupid, and it isn't completely rational. But, after years of being ignored by most of the guys in Juniper for being different, Trent had been the one guy who seemed to like me just as I was. The thing is, I had no idea he had a score card going and I was on that card. It wasn't anything worse than some other women deal with and I wasn't a virgin, but it taught me that I'm not relationship material. I have too much baggage, which he told me when he dumped me.

And he's right. I might be a-okay with sex, but intimacy is another whole thing. It is not something I want to have with anyone. Being vulnerable is just too much to ask of me.

"Whatever. Let me throw some clothes on and we'll head into work."

She sighs and I know she isn't done with me, but she'll let me go for now.

Not wanting to tempt Fate, I hurry back to my bedroom. Well, as fast as I move after crappy sleeping and throwing up first thing in the morning. I grab a pair of black jeans and one of my favorite T-shirts that reads *I don't have the energy to pretend to like you today.* It fits my mood most days, but especially today.

Once we get to work, I'm feeling fine, even if I do have a few moments of dizziness. Because of that, I make an appointment to see the new doc, but she can't see me until tomorrow. Best part about all of this is that Becca wants me in the back room away from people. That is my favorite place to be.

I pick up lunch from the diner for both of us. I use the excuse of needing fresh air to get out of the store and away from Becca. She's my sister from a different mister, but she can get a little too maternal if someone is sick. Normally, it's my brothers, and I enjoy the way she bothers them to rest and all that. Me, I don't need it.

I set her salad on the sales counter while she's talking on the phone—probably with her mom from the sound of it—and start back to the office. I walk by the Danvers cardboard cutout and stop. We got it during the last release month. It wasn't easy, but I wrangled some people I knew in New York to get it. It helped that Stan Lee had put in a good word for me.

I take a step back and keep my gaze trained on the life size Danvers. There is something so familiar about him, but I don't know what it is. I mean, he's almost faceless, but there are features about him, the nose…the shape of his chin…it makes me blink.

The room spins a little, but I take a few deep breaths and steady myself. It only takes about thirty seconds and I'm able to head back to my office so I can sit and eat.

By five in the afternoon, I'm bored and out of stuff to do. I wander out to the floor. It's a weekday so we aren't that busy. Being a Wednesday even more so because in Texas, that's church night. So, I decide to play the song that drives Becca crazy. I search through my playlist, then I link it with the music system. *Just a Girl* by No Doubt comes screaming to life and Becca jumps at the sound. She turns around and gives me a dirty look.

"Absolutely not."

"Aw, come on, Becca, I'm bored."

"You've had dizzy spells. No way."

I ignore her, of course, because I always do that when she tells me I can't do something. Hell, I do that when anyone does. It's my nature. And for the first time in days, I feel better, and I want to celebrate.

I climb up on top of the sales desk and start dancing. I ignore everything going on around me and just let loose.

"And do not do the superhero landing, Everly. I swear to all the holy unicorns, I will lose it."

Of course, I ignore her, and when the music crescendos, I do the flip and land on my feet. It's the other feet on the floor in front of mine that has me blinking.

11

QUINN

"Come on, Quinn. I bet Becca would love to meet you. And her partner."

I study my youngest brother and wonder what he's up to. He's being a little persistent on getting me to go up to Juniper Springs. That can only mean he has other objectives.

"Her partner?"

"I told you that they own the shop together."

Something cold blows through me. Carter is being awfully pushy about this. "You're not trying to set me up with a groupie, are you?"

I hate that part of my job. Since the explosion of everything Marvel and nerdy, groupies have become part of the scene. I do not want to have anything to do with a woman who wants to sleep with me because of my work. I know a lot of people who do, but it's just not for me. Besides, I have someone. Or I thought I did.

I check my phone again. Not like I couldn't hear the text tone I've given Everly. It's been over twenty-four hours since she's responded to a text. I was hoping we could meet up somewhere next weekend. After the trip to Ft Worth, we talked about it again, but for some reason she's ignoring me.

And yes, I know it's only been a day, but this is the longest we've gone without contact since we met.

"No. I mean, if you like her, by all means. But I haven't even met her. I've just met Becca and she's a cutie."

I toss him another sharp look. "No."

He studies me for a long time, then he throws back his head and laughs. Ugh, he's annoying. I check my phone again.

He grabs it out of my hand.

"Hey."

"You need to get out and quit waiting for Everly to text you."

Fuck. Carter seems like an easygoing guy who is too self-involved to notice anything. He notices everything. Doesn't mean I won't lie to him.

"I have no idea what you're talking about."

He sighs and shakes his head. Probably because I could hear the doubt in my voice. And even if I didn't sound so unsure, Carter would figure out a way to kick my ass.

"You're drawing again, and I peeked."

Fucker. He knows I don't like anyone to look at anything before I'm finished. But I'm not going to let him see how unnerved that makes me. I cross my arms over my chest and stare him down.

I don't say anything. He shakes his head in resignation again, and I grab my phone back from him. I suddenly realize I'm like Gollum and my phone is the Ring. It's pathetic, but at the moment, I don't know what else to do. Other than hire a private detective to find her. And that is *not* creepy at all.

Carter grabs his keys. "Listen, I promise I'm not trying to set you up. I only did that a couple of times."

Yes, and usually in the most embarrassing ways.

"That was before you met Everly and started getting it on the regular."

I say nothing. Absolutely nothing. I can't deny it without him catching me on it, and why should I deny anything. Everly is everything I could want in a woman. Strong and beautiful, with just enough sarcasm to keep me in line. If only she hadn't ghosted me a week ago.

"Did you draw her?"

I frown and cross my arms. "What do you mean?"

He can't know that I've created a character in her image. Okay, she might have her personality too.

"I knew it." He claps his hands together and gives me one of those stupid smiles of his that makes me want to smack his face. "You added her to your series. It's about time Danvers gets some. I mean, he's a surly bastard, just like you are when you aren't getting any. Remember when he got shot two books ago?"

"Of course I remember. I wrote it." Then it sinks in what he says. "You read my books?"

His smile fades as his eyes narrow. "Of course I do, bro. But promise me you're going to allow Danvers to get laid. And with your mysterious woman, Everly, right? What's her last name?"

I don't say anything for a long moment. "I don't know."

"Wait, what?"

"We didn't exchange last names. Her rule."

"Hmm, interesting. You've been kind of a bear today. Want to tell me why?"

I sigh and give up. He will eventually get it out of me or figure it out. "I haven't heard from her."

"What did you do?"

"Nothing." At least I didn't think I did. I played by her rules. Kept my thoughts inside the lines she drew. The fact that I itch to erase them and draw my own is a problem I am dealing with.

"Listen, who knows what could have happened, but let's get your mind off the issue. I want you to check out Becca's shop. It would be a great place to have a launch party."

"In Juniper Springs? Isn't that just a little town?"

Our oldest brother has a connection to the town through his girlfriend Sydney, who was raised there, but I haven't been there. My brothers had all made the trip when Syd and her best friend were arrested for disturbing the peace, but I had been on my way out of town to California. And Everly.

"Mon frier, let me tell you, people make pilgrimages there. Those two gals even got Stan Lee to come by for a visit a few years ago."

"Yeah?" I don't really want to go, but maybe Carter's right. A day trip might get me out of my head. And then I might be able to come up with another solution. "Fine. But I'm not going to be set up."

He holds his hands up in surrender. "Hey, this is just getting you out of town. I have the day off and I need a patty melt from the diner in town. You get to meet Becca and see if you can do a launch there. All good."

I know that there's more to it than that, but for the moment, I will play along for the distraction.

It doesn't take us long to get to Juniper Springs. It sits just an hour northwest of San Antonio. It looks a lot like other small towns in Texas, only a little more colorful. Rather than boring red brick stores lining Main Street, each store is painted a different color. One shop even has a rainbow flag hanging in front of it. Carter parks in front of Nerdvana and I smile. I step out of Carter's SUV and study the window. The display has a Marvel influence, that's for sure, but it's more whimsical than a lot of other stores. Whoever designed it is definitely artistic because while it hits the demographic to pull people in, it is bright and colorful.

"I told you," Carter says.

Yeah, he's a smug bastard, but he's right most of the time. And when it comes to marketing, no matter what the business, Carter is some kind of genius. It's a funky little town that might appeal to my readers and better yet, these women apparently also have a following. And if I'm introducing a female partner for Danvers, this might just be the right way to go for the launch.

"Okay, let's do this. I think I might need a patty melt myself."

"And a milk shake!"

Yes, he yells it like he's some kind of five-year-old making demands and not an adult with his own money.

We step into the store, and it's as if we stepped into another dimension. There is an explosion of color in every corner. My first impression is that it's a hodgepodge of things thrown together, but as I study it, I realize it is insanely organized by theme. The Marvel area has lots of blue and red, the DC area has lots of black...and then there's the graphic book area that includes a life size cardboard cut out of my character Danvers.

"Oh, wow, that looks a lot like you."

It does, but so does Elliot Danvers. I don't even try to hide the fact that I pour a lot of my own personality into him. I just make it ten times worse. Like when I got divorced, I killed off a woman he was interested in. It might have been passive aggressive, but it was cheaper than therapy.

"I wonder where they got it?" he asks.

I can barely hear him because Gwen Stefani's voice is blasting out from the speakers about being just a girl. That's when I see Everly. She's standing up on a counter dancing to the song. Part of me chuckles at the scene because it is *so* Everly. She does exactly what she wants when she wants.

Then it hits me.

Everly.

"Hey, isn't that—"

I walk away from Carter and march to the sales counter. My heart is beating so hard in my chest, I'm amazed I don't pass out. Seriously.

I hear another voice yelling at her. "And do not do the superhero landing, Everly. I swear to all the holy unicorns, I will lose it."

Everly ignores her. Instead, she gets to the crescendo of the song and does a flip off the counter, complete with a superhero landing with one knee and hand on the ground. My heart jumps into my throat and then plunges to the pit of my stomach.

A woman dressed as if she's going to Comic-Con comes rushing towards us, her worried expression telling me she was just as freaked out as I was.

"I told you not to—oh. Hello."

Everly rises up and when we make eye contact, hers widen in surprise. Everything in my entire being is focused on her. It's like my soul settles in a happy hum the moment our gazes connect. She shakes her head as if trying to figure out if I'm real.

Right there with you, babe.

"Quinn?"

"Yeah."

"Oh, I see you met Becca," Carter says forcing me to tear my attention away from Everly to the other woman. She's shorter by several inches, rounder, and her hair is blonde with blue tips. She's wearing a pink dress with unicorns all over it. She's also wearing a headband that has white ears and a white horn on it like she's a unicorn.

"Becca, this is my brother Quinn."

"Welcome to our store," she says, taking the skirt of her dress and giving me a curtsey. Maybe I hit my head and I'm in a coma. I sniff to check to see if I smell waffles since that is a sign of a stroke. That would explain running into Everly this way.

"That would make you the business partner," Carter

says. "I'm trying to talk him into doing a launch of the newest *Sharp Edges* book here. I think it would rock."

Everly owns a bookstore...one that apparently focuses on my genre.

"Wait. Your brother is Q. Hawthorne?" Becca exclaims.

But I pay no attention to her. I watch Everly, whose eyes widen again, then her face goes pale. The next thing I know, her eyes roll back in her head and she collapses. I rush forward and catch her right before her head hits the ground.

12

EVERLY

I'm only out for a few seconds, but when I wake up, I realize two things. I am being held by someone and that someone is Quinn.

"There you are," he says, relief coloring the edges of his deep voice.

I reach out and trail my fingers over his cheek. "What are you doing here?"

"I brought him. Brought him all the way up here."

I blink and look over and find his brother. "Why? What is actually going on? And you can put me down."

"That's okay. I think I'll hold on to you."

I have a feeling there is a double meaning in that comment, but I'm too dizzy to figure it out right away. Thinking makes my brain hurt right now.

"You need to go to a doctor. Even I know that," Carter says.

"I have an appointment tomorrow."

"Well, you need to go now," Becca says, but I pick up

on the tone in her voice. I glance over and realize that she's staring down at her phone.

"Why?"

"Apparently it's already been reported on the Juniper Springs Express. And you know as soon as Wyatt sees it, he'll be over here."

"Who the fuck is Wyatt?" Quinn asks.

I open my mouth to tell him to mind is own business, but Becca responds before I do. "Her brother. He raised her from the time she was twelve. He'll freak all the way out."

"It was just a dizzy spell, and we know why that happens."

"No. We don't, so maybe you should explain," Quinn says, his terse tone jolting me. He has never been surly or rude to me. But that tone...yeah, he's not happy right now.

I study him, and I know he would let me down if I insisted. But seriously, it feels too good to be in his arms again. He's big, and warm, and cuddly, even as he frowns at me. Which turns me on, but that's normal for me. Quinn's existence arouses me on a regular basis.

"I've had bouts of anemia."

The worried expression in his green gaze deepens. "Bouts?"

I shrug. "My mom had the same thing. It's treatable, but this hit me when I got hit with the stomach flu."

Then I hear Becca on the phone. She's too far away for me to hear what she's saying, but she's not on the phone long.

"Let's go," she says in a tone that is all business. "Dr. Abernathy couldn't fit you in, so you're going to the ER."

"Becca."

"She agrees you need to see a doctor. You need blood tests to be sure. You know all the normal stuff."

There is something in Becca's gaze as it moves back and forth between Quinn and me. I know all of Becca's looks, or I thought I did. This is one I can say I have never seen before. She's hiding something from me.

"I'm going with you," Quinn says interrupting my thoughts. I turn to look at him and my heart sighs. There is true concern in his eyes. He's so pretty and I want to stay right where I am in his arms. And that scares me more than fainting.

"You need to put me down first."

He hesitates, like he doesn't want to, but he does finally set me on my feet. My head is still spinning, but I can at least stand up without passing out.

"This has been fun," Carter says. "Definitely going to do a launch here."

I look over at Quinn's brother. He's just the same way I remembered him from Denver. Perfectly dressed, his hair styled in that way it makes it look like he hasn't had it styled, Carter's smiling at me much the same way he did that first night. The entire family is ridiculously gorgeous. Then his comment sinks in.

"What are you talking about?" I ask.

"Quinn is Q. Hawthorne."

I stop walking and look at Quinn. "You're Q. Hawthorne? No."

He doesn't respond so I look at Carter, who nods.

I look at Quinn with narrowed eyes. "Why didn't you tell me?"

"We said no last names, remember?"

I nod, as my mind starts to work through everything I know about Q. Hawthorne. He comes from a pretty rich family, but he has nothing to do with the business. He's been a monk for the last few years, and he never allows his publisher to put him on the cover. He apparently hates that. And I've been fucking him for the last few months.

My all-time favorite writer. Jesus.

"I'll catch up with you," Becca calls out. "I'll close everything up, then meet you all over there."

Quinn helps me to the car and sits in the backseat with me. I give Carter the address, and we hit the road. The truth is, for the most part, it takes no more than twenty minutes to get anywhere in Juniper except during the summer. Tourists are the worst.

My stomach protests and I close my eyes. I do not want to embarrass myself and barf all over Carter's SUV. Quinn apparently picks up on it and scoots over closer to me and wraps his arm around me. I close my eyes and settle my head against his shoulder, thankful for the comfort. Later I will be mad about it, but right now, it's the best thing in the world.

"Hey, we used to know a Dr. Abernathy. He was friends with Dad, right, Quinn?" Carter asks.

"Yeah."

"I guess it isn't him."

I snuggle closer to Quinn enjoying his warmth and

the unique scent of him. "No. It's a woman. She's new in town."

"Ah, well, that's good, because the Abernathy we knew was a proctologist."

I can't help it. I snort and my body relaxes further into Quinn as I feel his mouth brush over my temple. It's not sexual in any way, and I gladly take the comfort. For some reason I feel close to tears.

"I'm going to drop you off by the door, and then park. You shouldn't walk far," Carter says as he stops in front of the ER.

"You will not carry me in there."

Quinn frowns and I see that he wants to argue with me. He gets points because he apparently pushes those thoughts aside and nods. After helping me out of the SUV, he walks by my side into the ER. Everyone turns in our direction when we walk into the room.

"What's happening?"

I forgot that Quinn isn't from Juniper. How do I explain the insanity of how my hometown operates? It's odd even to me and I grew up here.

"It was on the JSE, an app that keeps the LOLs up to date."

"And they all just show up?"

I shrug because it's hard to explain our town. For a hippy kind of place, they have been trying to legalize pot for over a decade, they sure do like to get involved in our business.

"Take a seat, Ev," Margie, the receptionist and former classmate of mine says. "Oh, and fill this out. We should have the room ready in a second."

Quinn escorts me to a couple of chairs and we sit down. "What's JSE and LOLs?"

"Juniper Springs Express is an app that helps everyone keep up to date with everything going on in Juniper. The problem is that the LOLs, or Little Old Ladies, have started using it as some kind of giant gossiping thing. They stick their noses into people's lives and they out teenagers who are trying to sneak around. It's a nightmare."

"Ah, okay."

"You should take better care of yourself," Mrs. Petersen remarks.

"I think you should mind your own flipping business."

I know I'm horrible. I should respect my elders, but Mrs. Petersen is the queen bee of the LOLs. She was also the school librarian and a pain in my ass all through high school. Before she can respond, Margie calls my name. Quinn rises, but I shake my head. "Absolutely not. I got this."

"You're not family, are you?"

His gaze goes to Margie and I can practically feel her libido flutter to life. Anger shoots through me and I have to bite back on a growl. I step closer to him, because he's mine.

What the actual fuck? I don't take ownership of men, but I can't fight the need to snatch Margie bald-headed.

"No."

"Sorry. Only family for right now."

He takes both my hands and I look up at him. "I'll be right here."

I nod and follow Margie back through the labyrinth of hallways to the exam room.

After taking my vitals, Margie leaves me to change.

Doctor Denise, who used to be my pediatrician years ago, comes in. She's in her sixties, with short curly grey hair, thin as a rail, with kind blue eyes. We aren't a big town and most of the docs in town have emergency training to handle the things like this. They tend to take shifts at the emergency clinic. Anything major and people are sent to San Antonio or Austin.

"I'm sorry you had to wait."

"No problem."

She sits down on the little stool. "I see your blood pressure is a little high."

I nod.

"And the anemia is back?"

"I assume. I have an appointment tomorrow, but I passed out at work."

"Yes, I saw it on the JSE."

I mutter under my breath.

She offers me an understanding smile. "I want to take some blood for tests first. I see that you had a pap not too long ago, and I don't see a reason for any of that unless it isn't anemia."

I nod again.

"Sit tight and the tech will come take your blood, and I also want a urine sample. We will see what we have going on."

"You do all the testing in house?"

She nods. "We should have all the answers in less than an hour."

It's all relatively painless as I know the tech also. It's just this way in Juniper, which drives me crazy sometimes, but when I'm feeling like crap, it's a comfort.

After I've been in there for about forty-five minutes, there's a knock at the door. Then Becca sticks her head in.

"Hey, you're not family," I say smiling, my spirits lifting.

She gasps in that Becca way that makes me chuckle. "I should smack you for that."

"You've never hit anyone."

"Not true. I punched Ford one time when he said unicorns weren't real." Her brother got a love tap on the shoulder for that. She sits in the chair beside the bed. "But I *am* your sister."

"You are, in every way that counts. But how did you get back here?"

"Margie snuck me in the back way. She said a sexy Marvel superhero wanted back here and it was best that I come in that way."

I sigh and nod. "And why were you looking at me the way you were in the store?"

She opens her mouth, but Doctor Denise interrupts her. The sharp knock, then she comes in.

"Oh, hello, Becca. How are you?"

"I'm lovely, but I'm worried about Everly."

"Indeed." Her blue gaze swings my direction. "You are anemic, but since your form said you've been queasy—"

"What?"

We both ignore Becca's outburst. "I did a pregnancy test."

I blink. "I'm on the pill. And I always insist on a condom."

"Yes, well, not everything is one hundred percent. I read that you had an ear infection a couple months ago."

I nod.

"Some antibiotics can mess with your birth control."

After that, I don't really hear much of what she's saying. It's like she's in a tunnel a million miles away from me or maybe the teacher from the Charlie Brown specials. She's telling me that I need to go for an appointment—which I just said I have an appointment tomorrow—but instead of pointing that out, I just nod. Before I know it, I'm alone with Becca.

She doesn't look surprised. In fact, even though she has an air of sympathy about her, she also looks smug AF.

"You knew."

She shrugs. "I didn't make the connection until I saw you with Quinn. You've been so tired and yesterday you were complaining that your boobs hurt. Both signs of early pregnancy"

I close my eyes as the ramifications hit me hard. "Fuck my life."

"Are you okay?"

I swallow to prevent screaming out my response and open my eyes. Becca's aquamarine eyes study me with understanding and concern. "You're asking me that. I'm the one woman who shouldn't be a mother."

She frowns at me, looking very much like a disgruntled unicorn. "Why would you say that?"

"Becca, you know what I'm like." More than anyone she does.

She opens her mouth to argue, then apparently thinks better of it and snaps it shut. After she lets loose a long sigh, she says, "Right now, let's just concentrate on getting you out of here and home. You need to rest and maybe have some food. I'll have Mason bring you some of that broth you like when you're feeling under the weather."

"Okay."

I almost feel like crying, but I force the tears back by sheer will. I will not fall apart, even in front of Becca. If I did, she would freak out.

I get dressed quickly as Becca holds up my phone. "I got you an Uber and Margie is going to help us out the back way once you get your discharge papers."

It takes less than ten minutes once Becca starts in on the staff. The woman could be a general if they would let her wear a uniform with unicorns on it. She helps me to the Uber giving me a kiss on the forehead.

"I'll take care of everything in there," she says pointing to the hospital.

"I love you."

She smiles. "Right back at ya."

Then I am on my way. Sitting in the back of the Uber was probably not the best idea as he takes a turn faster than I expect. My stomach revolts, and I close my eyes, breathing through my mouth. I just hope that I make it home without embarrassing myself.

13

QUINN

The moment Becca steps into the waiting room, I know that something big happened. She's alone and my stomach plummets at that realization. There's no fear in her gaze, so my nerves settle just a little. Which tells me one thing that happened while she was back there. Becca makes her way over to us and before she can open her mouth, I take over the conversation. She punked out on me and ran out the back door, if ER's have back doors.

"Where does she live?"

Her eyes widen. "Uh, why would you want to know that?"

"She snuck out the back, right?"

She blinks, then studies me. A second later, her mouth curves and her entire expression lights up.

"She might not want you there."

"Too damn bad."

The giggle takes me by surprise, but I don't know why it does. Becca is definitely one of the happiest people I have ever met, even though I have only had a few short conversations with her.

"You'll do." She rattles off the address, then her gaze moves to the door. Two massive men walk through the door, broad chests, both at least an inch taller than me. But when I see their eyes, I see Everly.

"Go on. I'll take care of the boys."

"Are you sure?"

The older of the two takes notice of how Becca and I are leaning towards each other. His expression darkens as he stomps over to us. Something tickles at the back of my neck and I look around the room. It's then I notice that the entire room is watching us like we're a telenovela. It's like they know what's going to happen and they're all here for the show.

"Go on."

I take the coward's way out and follow Carter out the door, feeling the angry gaze of Everly's brother as we do. I know he probably wants to know what's going on with me and Becca, but he wants to find out what's going on with his sister more, so he doesn't follow us.

"Damn, those two could have broken you in half. I mean, you're a big guy, but...how did Everly get back to her house?"

The cool night air eases some of my anxiety. I have no idea why she ran away, but there is no way I am letting her slip through my fingers now that I found her.

"I have no idea. Maybe a ride share."

It doesn't take us long to get to her house. It's a rancher, probably built sometime in the last century. There's a massive porch and it looks well lived in.

"Do you mind waiting for me?"

"I do mind, but I will do it. You will tell me everything that happens while you're in there. EVERYTHING."

"No."

He sighs, shaking his head. "Fine. Then I'm going to go get a patty melt. Text me when you're done."

I slip out of the car and walk up the sidewalk to her front door.

"She doesn't like unannounced visitors," a voice calls out. I turn and find a tiny woman, somewhere between the age of sixty and one hundred. She's in a housecoat, her hair up in rollers, and she's drinking what looks like a dirty martini. She might look like she's dressed for bed, but she has a full face of makeup, including a bright orange red lipstick.

"Good to know."

I step toward the porch and she calls out, "Last time some man showed up here, she threatened to chop off the line and tackle. Don't say I didn't warn you."

I turn and watch her amble back to her house across the street. I shake my head. Small towns. I've never lived in one, and I have a feeling this one is a little different from most.

I step on the porch and have to wipe my palms on my jeans. Drawing in a deep breath, I knock on her front door. My stomach turns even as my dick jumps. It's a twisted feeling, and it's the same way I feel every time I'm about to see Everly.

At first, there's no sound and I think that maybe Becca punked me. But I hear Everly's footsteps approach the door. It swings open.

Just seeing her makes my soul vibrate. "What the hell are you doing here?"

She doesn't look any better than she did when we were at her store. "Becca gave me your address."

"Unfuckingbelievable."

"After I guessed that you ran away, she said I would do, then gave me your address."

She turns on her heel and stomps away, but she leaves the door open, and I take that as an invitation. Even if it isn't, I am not going to pass up my chance.

I step into her living area and instantly feel relaxed. That doesn't happen a lot because I tend to get a little antsy in someone else's space. The colors are cool, almost as if they were put together to soothe.

She plops down on a massive couch that looks more comfortable than my bed. "Well, what do you want, Q. Hawthorne?"

Sarcasm and distrust tinge her tone. "I didn't lie to you."

"You didn't tell me who you were."

Aggravation hits me in the chest, but I swallow back a retort. It's then I see the way her eye twitches just a little and the way she can't seem to meet my eyes now. There's something wrong, and it's bigger than what is going on between us. What if the doctor told her she's dying?

"What did the doctor say?"

Her eyes narrow. "You mean your new best friend Becca didn't tell you?"

"No. Your brothers showed up just as I was leaving though. Or I'm assuming they were your brothers."

"Big and stupid?"

I cock my head to the side and shove my hands in my pockets. It's that or grab her and pull her against me. I know that she would not like that at all.

"Do you not like any men?"

"Not really."

"What about me? You kept coming back for a reason."

Something I can't discern moves over her face, but it dissolves before I can figure it out. I'm used to her hiding things from me, but today, it just rubs me wrong.

"But I didn't know who you were."

"And that would have made it different?"

"Maybe."

"Besides, those were your rules, remember? No last names, no discussions of what we did for a living. I had no idea you had a comic bookstore, let alone one of the best ones in the Southwest."

"The best one this side of the Mississippi," she says with just enough arrogance it makes me smile.

"So, tell me, what happened at the hospital?"

She sighs as if it's the worst thing in the world. Oh, God, she *is* dying. We only had a short time together, but she's become so important to me. I didn't realize just how important until this moment.

"I'm pregnant."

The words hang there. It takes me a second to figure out just what she is saying. It's like I've lost the ability to understand the English language. I blink a couple of times trying to adjust from the idea that she's dying to the idea that she's pregnant. It's a whiplash for sure.

"Did you hear me? Quinn?"

I blink a couple more times, then look at her. She's

frowning at me, a look of concern darkening her eyes. I realize then she's waiting for an answer. I nod and plop down in the chair near me. I feel like I'm on a carousel after eating about five churros and chugging warm chocolate milk while Carter sings some kind of annoying song.

"Pregnant?" She nods. "We were careful."

"Yeah, and funny thing, I'm on the pill. But apparently, my medication for an ear infection made my pills null and void."

I don't say anything for a few moments, my brain cells trying to put together everything that just happened: From driving up here, finding her, to discovering I'm going to be a father.

That's when I notice her watching me. "What?"

"You aren't going to question if it is yours?"

I blink and study her. "I'm assuming it's mine."

Her entire expression seems to soften. "Good. Because it is."

I shove my hand through my hair. After my marriage fell apart, I pushed away the thought of kids. I figured with Gavin and Oliver adopting and now with Grady and Syd together, children would soon follow. I just thought I would be the cool uncle.

Who am I fooling? I've wanted kids for years and while my brain is still trying to catch up, a lightness I haven't felt in years—if ever—rolls through me. I'm going to be a father.

"What's that look for?"

"I...I'm hoping you're keeping the baby. I mean, I want you to but—"

WILD LOVE

"Yes. I never planned on having kids because I'm against relationships."

I ignore that last part. We'll deal with that when the time comes. "Good."

"And while I won't keep you from the baby's life, I don't require you to be here."

It takes me a second to compute what she's saying. When it does, irritation bubbles up, causing my tone to sharpen. "Excuse me?"

"I'm perfectly capable raising a child."

I realize then that she's serious. She's okay with me walking away and just leaving her on her own. Anger hits me hard in the chest. The idea that she wants to be without me to help hurts me on some level that even my marriage didn't get to. I just want to scream at her. I don't because she's carrying my baby.

Instead, I pop up out of my chair and pace. "So, I can just waltz out of the door and leave you alone to deal with this? What about financing the birth, school...all of that?"

She shrugs. "I can handle it."

I stop in front of her, my hands on my hips ready to let loose on her. She should be demanding I help with this, but it's almost like she expects me to be relieved.

As I study her, I realize it's all a lie. Or at least a half lie. I see the anxiety beneath the surface. She's picking at her leggings like she does when she's nervous. I've learned a few of her tells through our time together, and this is always the thing I notice her doing when she's worried about something. So, she isn't as sure as she's acting.

And right there, that's why I can't let her go, why I

don't think I ever will. I know she didn't want any ties, but each time we met up, I would find myself falling for her more and more.

I realize what she's doing, what she's been doing all along. The comment about relationships reminds me of all the rules she has about our relationship. I take her by the hand and tug her off the couch. I cup her face and kiss her. No holding back, just straight up kissing the hell out of her. When I pull back, I can barely breathe, and my entire body is urging me to throw her over my shoulder and march back to her bedroom. For her part, her face is flushed, need simmering in her gaze.

"I will definitely be around. A lot."

"Quinn." The warning tone in her voice doesn't faze me. Not now. I'm too happy. Nothing is settled, but now that I have a quest—to make this impossible woman fall in love with me—I'm determined.

"A lot, so you better get used to having me around."

She sighs again, but she nods. Then, I remember the last day when she didn't text me back.

"Did you know? Or have an idea? Because you didn't answer my texts."

She crosses her arms. "I didn't know. Seriously."

"Then why the radio silence?"

"Do we have to talk about this right now?"

No, we don't have to, so I should let it go.

"No, but we will come back to it."

"Great."

"I have to take care of a few things in San Antonio, then I will be back. Do you have room for me here? I guess I could crash with Nancy and Travis."

The stars of *Flipping Texas* work for my family, but they make their home here in Juniper. At least I'm sure Nancy has a place here in town. If not, there's got to be some rental properties in town.

"I have a guest room. But Quinn..."

I turn and look at her. "Get used to having me around, Everly."

The look she gives me should scare me. Instead, it's one of the looks I love to get from her. God, the woman has had my balls in her hands from the moment I saw her in Denver. That petulant look, the way she's eyeing me suspiciously...it gets me going. But right now, I need to make sure she understands how this is going to go. I step closer and slip my arms around her. I swallow her gasp as I slam my mouth down on hers. It's quick, hot, and my dick isn't happy when I step back from her, but I have things I have to get done.

"I'll be back tomorrow morning."

As I step out the door, I don't look behind me. Because what I wanted to tell her was that we were going to be together from this moment forward. I know she would fight me on it. And one thing my mom taught me was you pick your battles. My first battle is getting back here. I will worry about the rest of it later.

Me: *Come pick me up.*

Carter: *Who dis?*

Me: *Get your skinny ass over here right now.*

Carter: *If my ass is so skinny then I should finish this milkshake.*

Me: *Get it to go.*

Carter: *That isn't safe, drinking and driving like that.*

I roll my eyes and push back on my irritation. There's one thing that will get Carter moving and that's blackmail. If he hadn't spent his teen years being an asshole, we would have nothing on him. Thankfully, he's learned his lesson and treats women with more respect. Still, all three brothers have something on him, and we use it when we need to get him to do something.

Me: *If you don't pick me up, I'll tell Mom that you not only bagged both of the Reynolds twins at the same time, but you did it in her bed.*

Carter: *Be right there.*

"I see you survived," I hear a voice call out across the street. I glance over and notice the same woman who accosted me on the sidewalk, but she's not alone. There are several women with her, and they seem to be having a party of some sort. They all have their phones out as if they are checking out...shit, I don't know what a bunch of old women would be doing on their phones. It makes me just a little uncomfortable, since it looks like they are aiming them at me. That is until they all drop their hands and look a little guilty. I frown.

"Hey, stud," Everly's neighbor says, drawing my attention back to her. She has the same glass in her hand, but I'm pretty sure it's a fresh drink.

I offer her a smile. "I just got the best news in the world, and I'll be here a lot from now on."

"Is that a fact?" she asks, as her companions start whispering. I ignore them and just nod, then start off down the street, thinking that the sooner I meet up with my brother, the faster I can get back to Everly.

14

EVERLY

I lay on my couch, a glass of water on the coffee table and a bag of milk chocolate chips on my chest. Don't judge me. I already said I wasn't built to be a mother. And it's been kind of a bad day. I know I won't be able to avoid my family, so I need my chocolate. Becca must be doing something to keep my brothers away. She's sweet but she's protective of me. I also know that she can keep them away for only so long.

My phone buzzes on the coffee table and I pick it up. I've been ignoring it for a while. Apparently, the JSE found out about my illness and it's all anyone can talk about.

Becca: *We're almost there.*

Oh, shit. I sit up and drop my bag of chocolate next to my glass of water. I go through all the missed texts and realize that she's been keeping my brothers away.

They started about an hour ago.

Wyatt: *Becca said you were okay, but I need a text.*
Wyatt: *No, I need a call.*

Mason: *Call Wyatt or he's going to start busting heads.*

Five minutes after that:

Wyatt: *I swear to the tiny baby Jesus if you don't call me, I will be busting some heads.*

I would laugh if I wasn't still in shock. Then, there was a series of texts from Becca.

Becca: *Don't be mad at me about Quinn. He was worried about you.*

Becca: *Oh, crapola. You made the JSE. There was a mention of a gentleman caller.*

God, Jon Howard should be shaved and marched through the town naked for inventing that app. Lucky for him that he lives in California. I look it up and find the one Becca texted about.

Juniper Springs Express: *Hey, just so everyone knows, Everly is at home and feeling better. Even had a gentleman caller.*

Wyatt: *Who the hell is this gentleman caller?*

Mason: *Dude, who you banging?*

Oh. My. God. My brothers are both horrible.

Before I can text back, there is banging at the door.

"Open up, Everly. I know you're in there."

Ugh, Wyatt. I could handle Mason, but Wyatt is like my dad in a lot of ways. He's ten years older and raised us after our parents died. I sigh and pull myself off the couch.

When I open the door, I find both of my brothers standing there, blocking my view of the street.

"Move it or lose it, Spencers," Becca bellows. Startled by her voice, both of them jump out of her way. Immediately, she wraps her arms around me, which isn't that strange for Becca, but she knows how I feel about too many hugs. Still, it feels pretty good.

"I haven't told them about the test and everything. Thought you might want to wait," she whispers in my ear.

Okay, so she had a plan. I nod, but I hold onto her a few more seconds. When she steps back, my brothers come in.

"So, you didn't call us when you got sick?" Wyatt asks as he settles his hands on his hips.

"She passed out, dude. She couldn't call," Mason says shaking his head. He ignores my rules about hugs and gives me one.

I pull back and look at Wyatt. "What Mason says. I thought Becca called you." He frowns and crosses his arms over his chest. "And yes, I should have called you when I got there. Sorry."

His gaze softens. "We were worried, Evie."

He's the only one who uses my childhood nickname. And every time he does, it gets me emotional. It always reminds me of my father, who gave me the nickname. And usually, I can keep it controlled. But apparently, the demon seed causes me to lose complete control. It's that or the day has just been a little too much.

Tears fill my eyes, and they pour down my face. My brothers are not accustomed to me crying and both of them panic.

"Oh, damn, Evie, kiddo," Wyatt babbles as he pulls me into his arms. I hold on tight remembering all the times he did this for me when I was younger, in those days after we lost both of our parents and he had to change his whole life for us. He never complained and he was always there for me. And I have to tell him I'm pregnant by a man I barely know. He might not be my father, but he is the surrogate.

"You didn't tell us it was bad."

"Don't take that tone with me, Wyatt Bartholomew Spencer," Becca says. "And it's not bad, but it's been a long day."

I pull back. "Let's all go into the living room and get this over with."

Everyone files into the living room. My brothers sit on the couch and Becca takes the overstuffed chair that Quinn sat in.

"So, I might have anemia again. But that's not the biggest thing that's wrong with me."

"It's not wrong, just not what you expected," Becca says, the gentleness almost making me cry again. I hold myself together. Jesus, if this is how the pregnancy is going to go, I already hate my kid. And right there is the reason I shouldn't be having children.

I look at both of my brothers, who are equally worried, Wyatt more so because it's his nature and it's been his job for years. Yes, I am an adult woman who can handle her life, but Wyatt will always worry like a parent because he acted as ours from the time our parents died.

I glance at Becca, who nods and smiles, letting me know that no matter what, she's going to be here.

"I'm pregnant."

There is a beat of silence, then both of my brothers seem to release a breath. The sound is rather loud in my quiet house.

"Thank God," Mason says. "We were both convinced you were dying."

"You're not mad?" I ask, keeping my gaze on Wyatt.

He shakes his head. "I mean, I thought you never wanted kids."

"I didn't."

"It's better than you dying, though. That I couldn't handle," he says, rising and hugging me again. He gives me a kiss on the forehead.

"I thought you would be disappointed."

He frowns down at me. "What? Why?"

"I'm not married and I'm pregnant."

"And this is the twenty-first century and fuck anyone who says anything to you."

"Told ya," Becca says. I smile over at her. Before I can respond, Mason grabs me out of Wyatt's arms and hugs me again. I'm really going to have a talk with my brothers about this, but today, I accept it. I need this warmth from the two people who know me better than anyone except Becca.

"I have some broth in the truck. I'll go get it." He kisses the top of my head and heads out to get it.

"Sit down, Everly. We need to talk," Wyatt says.

Ugh, this is what I didn't want to do today.

"Can this wait?"

Wyatt shakes his head. "We need to talk about your choices."

"First of all, I know my choices, and second of all, I already decided to keep the baby."

He nods, but he looks at the couch. I roll my eyes and sit down. Becca comes over to sit next to me.

"What Wyatt is trying to say is that he supports you through this."

"I don't need you talking for me, woman."

I roll my eyes. Usually, I love to tease both of them about their animosity. At some point, they need to just fuck, but they've been playing this game for about two years. Tonight though, I'm tired and stressed and I just want to go to bed.

"I'm gonna heat this up. You stay there," Mason calls out as he heads into the kitchen.

"Shouldn't you be at work?"

"Took some personal time."

Then he ducks into my kitchen. It's a big thing when any of us take time for ourselves. We all own our own businesses and understand that means you sacrifice part of your personal life for it. For him to take off tonight just on the fly is a huge thing.

I look at Wyatt and open my mouth, but he shakes his head. "Don't even say anything. Stacey can handle it tonight. This is more important, and she has no problem since the whole fucking town knows about your trip to the ER."

I sigh and lean back against my comfy couch, sinking into the cushions and closing my eyes. "That fucking app."

Becca takes my hand. "You don't need to make all the decisions tonight. But I'm assuming you told Quinn?"

I nod my head and open my eyes. "Yeah."

"That's the gentleman caller?" Wyatt asks, the softness in his voice disappearing in a second.

I nod and he says something under his breath.

"Wyatt, let up on her," Mason says as he brings me a bowl of his bone broth, handing it to me. "There is extra in the fridge and I'll bring more by tomorrow if you do well with it."

I nod and sip the soup carefully. It's our mother's recipe, the only one she could cook well. Mason dug out all of the old cookbooks in storage. It reminds me of her, of the way she would always make this when we were sick. I miss her so much right now because she would understand. A family of men just doesn't understand this, and I need my mom more than anything right now. Tears fill my eyes again.

"Stop that," Wyatt orders, panic filling his voice.

"You stop," Becca says, slipping her arm around my shoulders and pulling me closer to her. "I'm going to go get some stuff and spend the night, so you don't have to be alone tonight."

"Where's the guy who knocked you up?" Mason asks and he puts his feet up on my ottoman.

"Seriously, asshole?" I ask, even as I slurp down some more broth. "Be nice or I won't tell you about him."

Being the youngest always gave Mason that fear of missing out.

"Fine."

"His name is Quinn and I met him in Colorado."

"That was over three months ago," Wyatt says. I look over at him. Of course, he would pay attention to it. Like when he kept a calendar of my menstrual cycle when I was in high school.

"Then I met up with him in California."

"Wait," Mason says, dropping his feet to the floor with

a thunk and leaning forward. "You met up with him again? Isn't that against *the rules*?"

"Yeah. But...he was just so nice. And he speaks geek."

"He also looks like Thor and Captain America had a baby," Becca says with a smile.

Wyatt's attention moves to Becca. "The guy who was slobbering on you at the ER?"

I raise an eyebrow at the tone.

"He wasn't slobbering. He was looking for Everly and needed her address."

Wyatt's gaze comes back to me. "And you were avoiding him why?"

"How do you know I was avoiding him?"

He sighs, sounding decades older than he actually is. "Because that's what you do, Everly."

True story. "Not true."

He sighs again, but it ends with a chuckle. He knows me too well. "Listen, I just need to know about this guy and if he's going to step up."

"I don't need to be married or have a life partner to raise a child."

"No. But it makes it easier. I'm sure Mrs. Gold would agree with me. Kids are expensive."

Becca snorts. "That won't be a problem."

Wyatt's gaze moves between us. "Okay. What is up with the guy?"

"And do we need to kick his ass?"

Everyone ignores Mason.

"We met in Denver, like I said, but he actually lives in San Antonio."

"Is someone going to tell me this guy's full name." Oh, great, he's using his 'I'm going to bust heads' voice again.

I nibble on my bottom lip and Becca, who hates tension and hates holding onto secrets, blurts out, "He's part of the Hawthorne family."

"The ones who paid for Syd's fight night?" Wyatt asks.

My lips twitch. "Yeah."

"And he was here because you thought you might be pregnant?"

I shake my head. "It was all an accident. He came up here with his brother to check out Nerdvana, not knowing that I owned it."

"And why would he do that?"

I sigh. "He's Q. Hawthorne."

"Why does that sound familiar?" Mason asks out loud.

"He writes *Sharp Edges*. The guy who is your favorite author is the baby daddy?" Wyatt asks, his tone turning incredulous.

"I didn't know it at the time. We didn't exchange last names."

"Why the fuck not?"

"My rule. Quinn is a bit of a..."

"Stalker?"

"Shut up, Mason," we all say at the same time.

"I could tell he was into long relationships. I'm not made for that. I thought it best."

"So, have your cake and eat it to?"

My shoulders sag. "No. Maybe."

Becca, who, as I said earlier, knows me better than anyone, takes control of the situation. "Listen, I think we need to talk about this tomorrow or later. Is Quinn coming back tomorrow?"

I nod. "I think so. He said he would be back and would be sticking around."

"There. So, I'm going to go get my stuff, your brothers will behave until I get back or I will tell Rhonda Cullen that both of them want to date her."

"Becca," Wyatt growls. Rhonda is my nemesis for good reason. She's just an awful person. I punched her out when she called Becca a bastard in school because Becca's biological father wasn't around. Pretty doesn't always mean nice.

"Promise me."

Both of my brothers promise. She gives me a one-armed hug, then she flits out the door. Wyatt takes her place on the couch.

"So this guy is kind of nice. Wait...he's a Hawthorne? As in the billionaire family?"

I nod.

"And he's coming back. Do you know that for sure?"

"Oh, yeah. He said he would stay somewhere else or with me. Either way, he would be here for me."

"Still," he grumbles.

"I know you want to make him hurt for some odd reason, but there's no need. He is all about me and the baby. I only saw him for about ten minutes, but he made sure that I knew he would come back."

"You two are arguing when we should be happy."

We both look over at Mason.

"We are going to have a baby to spoil. And me, I can't wait."

"Yeah," Wyatt says, his voice sounding lighter as he slings an arm over my shoulders. "We have another little Spencer on the way and that seems like an amazing thing."

For a second, I look at both of them and then I burst into tears.

"Aw, fuck, Everly, I'm sorry," Mason says. "It's going to be a long nine months if this is what happens when we say things that upset you."

Wyatt wraps his arm around me and pulls me into his side. "Don't worry, Evie. We'll get through this."

"Yeah, but will we survive?" I ask, half joking, half serious. "I mean, you remember how bad Mason was as a baby?"

He chuckles. "Yeah, but we'll have fun. And what do you know? You might have a baby girl. You always wanted a sister."

"I have a sister."

"True."

"How about we watch Marvel until Becca gets back?" Mason offers.

I smile at him, my heart softening. Neither of them is into Marvel like I am. His offer warms my heart. They might be idiots, but they are my idiots.

"Sure."

Mason gets me some more broth. We settle on the couch, my brothers on either side of me, as we watch *End Game*.

15

QUINN

I'm just about packed when my doorbell rings. That's not a good sign. It's six in the morning—way too early for me to be up, but I couldn't sleep. All I could think about was getting back to Everly. It's kind of like the times I was with her. I always felt hollow that first time back in my own bed.

The doorbell rings again and then there's knocking. And of course, shouting. Because...Carter.

"Open up, mon bro!"

I really need to get some kind of gate or something for my property.

I take my time zipping up the suitcase and taking it to the living room. When I open the door, I'm not happy at seeing Carter. I'm even less happy that both Sydney and Grady are there too.

"What the fuck, Carter? You promised to keep your mouth shut until I talked more with Everly."

"Believe me, we weren't happy when he showed up

last night," Grady says, stepping into my house without invitation. Sydney steps up.

"Oh, you didn't sleep well, did you?" She gives me a hug, which makes Grady growl. We pull apart and both of us roll our eyes. She joins Grady, leaving Carter standing on my porch.

"I guess this is all your fault, and I might kill you if you even thought about telling Mom and Dad."

He looks offended, like he didn't just drag Grady and Syd to my house at the asscrack of dawn.

"I would never do that. I mean, I don't want to be the one to tell them you knocked someone up."

It's my turn to growl, but he ignores it, giving me a big hug.

"I'm going to be the best uncle."

Of course, he's thinking about what this means to him.

I shut the door and join them in the kitchen. Syd is already making coffee, because that's Syd. She's a nurturer in a lot of ways.

"This girl," Grady starts but Syd interrupts whatever he was about to say.

"Everly," Syd says as she punches the coffee to brew, "is not a girl. She's a woman and a damned good one."

It's then that I remember Syd knows her from growing up in Juniper. "How well do you know Everly?"

"Pretty well," she says, leaning against the kitchen counter. "Her older brother Wyatt was a few years ahead of me. Everly a few years behind me. Oh, and Mason. He's the baby."

"He doesn't look like a baby. He was at the ER last

night. He's huge, but not as big as the older one," Carter says. He and Grady are sitting at the counter.

"Wait, Wyatt? The one who owns the bar?" Grady asks.

"Yes," Syd says.

"He's the one who raised them?"

She nods.

"Where were their parents?" Carter asks.

"They died when Everly was...I think around twelve. Car accident. Wyatt was actually making a name for himself on the bull riding circuit at the time and had to quit that and come back to Juniper full time. He sold the family farm and with the help of the Golds—those are Becca's parents—and he opened the bar and grill. You know Becca. She dresses like she's always ready for Comic-Con."

"Curtsies when she meets you?" Grady asks.

She nods with a smile. "They really are the two sweetest women. I mean, people don't see it with Everly, but she is."

"She hides it," I say.

Syd nods. "As much as I love Juniper Springs, it's not easy growing up in a place like that if you don't like to conform. And yes, it's more accepting, but remember, this was fifteen years ago. It couldn't have been easy on her. She also hates pity, so being one of the Spencer kids who lost their parents was hard to deal with, I'm sure."

I nod.

"What are your plans? And are you sure she didn't know about your family money?"

I look at Grady as anger shifts through my body,

heating my blood. It takes me a second or two before I can speak without yelling. "I love you, but if you say anything like that again about Everly, I will cut you out of my life."

He blinks, and I don't blame him. I have never been that confrontational. I'm the easy-going brother, the one who would rather be left alone.

"We didn't exchange last names, and she's the woman from Denver."

Carter raises his hand. "I picked her. I want credit."

"Shut up," both Grady and I say, and we share a smile.

"What's the plan?" Grady asks.

"Go up there. Stay."

Grady frowns. "I mean about the baby, your relationship, all of that?"

"Jesus, Grady, we just found out we live less than an hour away from each other and we finally shared our last names. She was exhausted and stressed last night. I felt it was better to give her space for a day, let her come to terms about the changes in her life."

I know she needed some time to think and that is all I did last night. I would marry her in a second. I know it's stupid, but from the moment I met her, I felt connected to her on a level that I have never felt with another woman —not even my ex-wife. Abby was a deterrent to my work.

I push aside thoughts of my ex. "And you're just moving up there without telling Mom and Dad."

"I planned on telling them. I just need to talk more with Everly and see which way this is going."

"You're going up right now?" Syd asks.

I nod and take the cup of coffee she made. God, she

makes the best coffee. I'd planned on grabbing something on the go, but this is much better.

"Then we all go."

This comes from Carter and sends a jolt of alarm through my entire body.

"No."

"Yes! I didn't get pie from the diner because you made me pick you up."

"You had a milkshake."

"That's a drink and not dessert."

It's annoying that he can eat anything he wants and stay slim. "You are not riding up with me. You need a ride back."

"Syd and Grady can take me back."

I glance at them and realize they're wearing casual clothes on a Thursday morning. "What's going on here?"

Grady opens his mouth, probably to complain, but Syd steps forward to take over. "Carter was really worried about you last night; said you wouldn't talk to him about it, and he wants to be there to support you."

Looking at Carter, who is inspecting his fingernails as if he doesn't have a care in the world, I know it's all an act. Truth is, he probably works just as hard as anyone in the family. And he is deeply attached to all of us.

"Fine, but I'm driving so I pick the music."

Of course, that lasts about five minutes before Carter takes it over and picks what he wants. It's just easier and my mind is on other things, like the fact that Everly texted me back last night, but there wasn't the usual edgy humor to the messages. Yes, I know that she just found out she was pregnant, but it still has me worried.

"I like Everly."

I blink and look over at Carter.

"What?"

"I like Everly. She's really good for you. Like when you were dating Elsa, she never fit. You know? Like Oliver fits in with our family and Syd too. Everly will fit."

I roll my eyes. "How do you figure?"

"She compliments you. She's edgy. You're a big teddy bear."

"What the hell are you talking about?"

Okay, so I just said her humor was edgy, but I am not a teddy bear.

"Yin and yang. The best of everything comes together and just works. That's you and Everly. And because of that, she will fit in with us like Elsa never did."

Carter is right about that. No matter how many times I tried to get her involved with the family, Elsa, fuck, no, her name is Abby. She just never fit in with the family. She was the one person who broke the rule about phones at the dinner table and ignored Mom's pointed stares.

"And, well, the baby isn't going to hurt. Mom is going to be over the freaking moon. And the best thing is that your baby and Oliver and Gavin's baby will get to grow up together. It's perfect."

Actually, that *is* a good thing. When we take the exit to Juniper, I feel my entire body start to relax. The town is just coming alive as I turn down her street. I park in the street and Grady pulls up behind me. The women who were out the night before are nowhere to be seen, but as I step out of my car, I notice there's a couple of mallards in the front yard. From the coloring, I can tell they are both males, which is odd because it's mating season. They are standing in front of Everly's front door quacking like it's the end of times.

"I had no idea they were still around," Syd says as she steps up beside me.

"What the hell is happening?"

"That's Bert and Ernie, so named by Everly. They showed up a couple years ago."

I look at her. "Two male mallards who hang out together?"

"I think they were calling them the Ambiguously Gay Duo, but thought Bert and Ernie was better."

"Gay ducks?"

She shrugs. "Juniper Springs is open to all lifestyles and sexualities."

I can tell she's trying her best to keep from laughing.

Before I can respond, Everly's door opens, and bread comes flying out. "I swear to God if you don't leave, after this, I am going to serve roast duck for dinner tonight."

Then her eyes widen at the group of us. She's wearing an old t-shirt and sleep shorts. Her hair is sticking straight up on one side, and there are still creases on her face from her pillow. My heart does that little jig it always does the moment I catch sight of her.

"Uh, what's going on?"

I ignore my family and walk toward her, up the steps. She watches me the entire time, her gaze never leaving mine. A sense of calm flows through me as I stop in front of her. She smells of jasmine and I just want to pull her into me, but I know that would be a mistake.

"I texted you."

She sighed. "I had to turn off my phone. Too many notices from the JSE."

I nod. "You need to rest. It's early."

"But you were going to show up here? I mean, how were you going to get in?"

I lean closer so I can whisper loud enough for only her to hear. "I was going to talk you into taking a nap with me because I didn't get any sleep either."

When I pull back, her lips are parted just a bit and I can tell I surprised her. I want to lean in, brush my mouth over hers, take her completely in, then scoop her up in my arms and take her to bed.

"No dice because my idiot brothers are coming over here this morning."

"I take it they know."

She sighs as she nods.

"I think we should all go inside. The LOLs are taking notice," Syd says from behind me. I look around and notice the woman from last night standing in her window watching us. Jesus.

I nod and wait for Everly to step over the threshold. I hold the screen door open for Syd, then I step in front of Grady, releasing the door and letting it hit Grady in the face.

"Asshole," he mutters, and I hear Carter laugh.

I'm smiling as I step into the kitchen. Everly is watching me again.

"What?"

Her cheeks turn pink as she shakes her head and mutters to herself, then turns to get mugs down from the cupboard.

"I told you I would take care of everything," Becca says as she walks in. She has her golden hair in a high ponytail, and she's dressed all in pink and white. She looks like…Barbie. She even has the old-fashioned makeup of the first Barbie.

"Oh, we have guests. Hello, everyone. Syd!" She rushes forward and hugs Sydney. "I'm so happy you're here."

Everly is reaching for one last mug, and I walk over, getting it down for her, then I say, "Take a seat. I can do the coffee."

"I can make coffee."

"I didn't say you couldn't, but you didn't sleep last night. Go relax."

She hesitates, then says, "Thanks. And I want to tell you right now, I'm sorry."

"For what? You didn't do anything."

"Yeah, but I'm related to those two idiots," she says motioning toward the kitchen window that looks out front. Her brothers have arrived, and they do not look like they want to be part of any welcoming party.

16

EVERLY

There are too many people in my house. I mean, it was bad before my brothers just showed up. Now though, I feel as if there is an army of freaking ants dancing over my flesh.

"Who the fuck are you?" Mason says, his gaze directed at Quinn. I move in front of him. I know that Quinn can handle himself. While he might be a big ol' teddy bear who gives the best hugs, I know that he could probably beat up at least one of my brothers. They are big guys, but so is Quinn.

"Mason Marshall Spencer!" Becca exclaims.

"That's not my middle name," he says, but his gaze stays on Quinn.

"Don't make me call Mama," Becca warns.

Mason does pull his attention from Quinn. "Don't do that."

"I will tell her you were mean to Quinn, and then she will let you have it."

"No. Okay. I'll be nice."

I have no idea what control Becca's mom has over Mason, but there's something there. He's always been connected to her since he was just ten when our mother died. It's like he could care less if the rest of us are mad at him, but his world would fall apart if Mrs. Gold had a bad thought about him.

"Good morning, Wyatt. Remember to use your words."

He frowns at Becca. "What's up with you this morning?"

I want to ask the same thing, but Becca just shakes her head.

Wyatt has a short stare down with her but loses as usual. "So, I guess you're Quinn."

I see Syd shake her head. "Cool your jets, Wyatt. Why don't we all take a seat and Everly and Quinn can fill us in?"

As we're walking into the living room, Carter decides to pipe up. "I just want to say of all of the brothers, I'm sure Mom and Dad thought I would be the one to knock someone up."

"Carter!" This comes from Syd, Grady and Quinn.

I have a feeling that is going to be something I hear in my sleep. Quinn is so angry at his brother and I try not to laugh, but, well, there's a reason they might fit into my family. My brothers are assholes too.

Once everyone is seated, Syd motions for me to talk. Although, all of a sudden, I can't talk. I feel everyone watching me and I can't form words. Worse, my stomach is starting to turn over again.

Quinn apparently senses it, taking my hand in his.

"We met in Denver when we went up there a few months ago. Then we met up in California a couple of months ago."

"And Ft. Worth a couple weeks ago," I remind him.

Wyatt looks at me, then turns his attention back to Quinn. "And you're just now getting around to coming to town to meet her family."

"I didn't know her last name."

Oh, if looks could kill, Quinn would be dead. I see Wyatt flexing his fists, probably contemplating how he wanted to break Quinn's nose.

"Not my rule," he says, causally. "That was Everly's."

Wyatt's gaze swings to mine and he frowns harder.

"Everly," Mason says.

The admonishment in his voice pisses me off. I'm tired from the no sleeping thing, and there are all kinds of people in my house. Like more people than have been in it for the last six months and they are all here at once. So, I am a little crazier than normal. It takes all of my control not to kick my brother in the balls for judging me. Also, we covered all this shit last night. And what gets me is they both know about this. They know I have my rules about relationships. I have never hidden it from them. But now that I'm pregnant, they think they can pass judgement? Screw that.

"Yeah. And tell me, Mason, when ya gonna bring a girl home for me to meet? Huh? I bet you knew every woman's last name and whole back story before you banged her."

He shakes his head. "You should know better."

Oh, he did not say that. I start to say something to

him, but it's all forgotten when the edges of the room seem to darken, and I sway.

Quinn is on his feet and wrapping his arm around me before I can pass out again.

"First of all, Everly can speak for herself, but both of you need to take a fucking step back. She hasn't been feeling well, and you're adding to the issue. Secondly, Everly has every right to her own private life and unless both of you are virgins, you can fuck right off."

I blink at the hardness of his voice, amazed that this is Quinn saying this. He's usually easygoing, but I believe my brothers pissed him off.

"I have to agree with Quinn," Becca says, which earns her a sharp look from Wyatt. She ignores him. "Plus, they just found out. All of us have invaded Everly's space. We know she doesn't like this many people in her house at one time, but here we are, crowding her and Quinn. They have a lot to talk over, none of it is any of our business, by the way. So, I suggest we go to the diner and grab a bite to eat."

"Milkshakes!" Carter yells.

"Carter, it's breakfast," Syd says.

"And I am an adult."

"That's debatable," Grady murmurs.

I can tell my brothers don't want to go, but they know better than to ignore Becca. She's already threatened them with her mother.

They all file out, but not before I get a hug from Sydney—this is getting out of hand—who says to text her if I need anything. Both of my brothers hug me again—ugh—and then Becca is the only one left with us.

"Now, you two talk things through. Or don't. You look like you could use a good long nap." She wraps her arms around me. "I know you hate hugs, but I can't help it."

"I know."

"I love you. And be nice to Quinn," she whispers in my ear.

I nod but say nothing as she pulls back. She looks at Quinn. "I can make you disappear on my family's ranch, so don't make me angry."

"Okay." Quinn's tone tells me he isn't taking her seriously. Kind of hard to when she's got her Barbie on.

"Becca!" Wyatt bellows from outside. She rolls her eyes.

Then takes her time to walk out the door, muttering under her breath.

The door shuts with a decisive click. We're left staring at each other.

"Sorry about my family," he says.

"Same."

His mouth curves just enough to make his dimple pop. God, he's gorgeous. And if I thought I was over him, I was mistaken.

Not that I have to get over him, especially now that I'm carrying his demon seed.

"What is going on in that beautiful head of yours?"

I blink and realize I spaced out for a minute or two. "Sorry. I've been a little spacey lately."

He nods. "Why don't you sit down? Yesterday was a long day and today started off with gay ducks, and all of us invading your sanctuary."

I would argue, because that's who I am. You tell me to

do something that is probably the best thing for me, I will disagree with you. It's a sickness. I know this, and I have had issues with it in the past. But let's be honest. We're all fucked up.

"Everly," he says, the gentleness in his voice piercing through the armor I erected over the years. I finally focus on him again. "Are you okay? Do we need to go back to the ER?"

I shake my head. "I'm so tired."

He nods. "Want anything to eat? Drink?"

"There's some bone broth that Mason brought over. It's in the fridge.

"You got it." He kisses my forehead. "Go on. Have a seat and let me take care of you this once."

I want to argue with him, but he's right. I'm exhausted. I sit down and he goes to get my broth. I lay my head down as my phone starts buzzing.

I pick it up and, of course, it's Becca's running commentary about what is happening.

Becca: *Your brother is being a total A-HOLEY.*

Becca: *I wanted to ride with Syd and Grady to catch up with Syd, but Wyatt almost had a meltdown.*

Me: *He's jealous, babe.*

Becca: *As if. He's just mad because I told him to not stick his nose in your relationship with Quinn.*

I hear Quinn moving around in the kitchen and I smile. Okay, I'll admit that I don't like guys at my house. Hell, the only person I usually like over is Becca, well, and her mother. My brothers are allowed over only every once in a while. But there is something about having

Quinn here, puttering around in my kitchen, making something for me to eat.

Becca: *What's happening?*

Me: *Nosey.*

Becca: *Come on. Both of your brothers have stopped talking to me.*

Me: *Quinn is heating some of the bone broth up for me.*

Becca: *Aww, that's sweet. Do you still want me to go to your appointment with you?*

Me: *I'll let you know.*

"So, is Carter behaving?" Quinn asks me as he brings in a bowl of soup. He has a thick kitchen towel beneath it to keep me from burning my hand.

"Yeah. I guess. They haven't gotten there yet, but I'm assuming with Carter in the car, anything is possible."

He nods as he lifts my feet, takes their place on the cushion, then sets them on his lap. The intimacy of the moment would normally have me running in the other direction. Instead, this makes me feel…relaxed. It's odd because only with those people I truly love do I feel like this. And even with some of those people—mainly my idiot brothers—I feel a little out of sorts if they are in my space.

Quinn is different. It's like he fits here in my house, with me. And I should be scared because I don't do feelings. I do one-night stands. Feelings don't enter into the equation. Usually.

"Eat."

I blink at him.

"I mean, I know I'm pretty, but you need to eat," he says, as he offers me the cutest lopsided grin I've ever seen. Listen, I know it's overused, but that's just what it is—complete with that cute little dimple. And I want to see it more. I want to be the person who makes him this happy.

He looks down at the bowl, then up at me. I smile and start spooning the broth into my mouth. The savory liquid dances over my tastebuds and then warms my belly. God, Mason is such a good chef. I hum as I take another spoonful.

"That good?"

I nod. "He's an idiot, but the boy can cook."

He settles back against the couch and takes one of my feet into his hands and starts rubbing it.

"Do you mind if I go to your appointment with you?"

My knee-jerk reaction is to say no. I do things on my own, except that first time when Becca's mom took us to our first exam. This is different though. This little alien inside of me is part Quinn and I guess the father's usually go.

"No. You should be there."

His shoulders relax and I realize he was waiting for me to deny him the privilege.

"And this anemia?"

The worry in his voice catches my attention. "I've had issues with it in the past. But from what I was reading, I'll be put on iron supplements. All expectant mothers usually are."

He nods and picks up my other foot and starts rubbing it. The action relaxes me further. It's all so normal, so mundane and wonderful at the same time. Having him treat me like a goddess should freak me out.

No. Not being treated like a goddess. Every woman should get that. It's how much I love it, how I would be perfectly happy to sit there all day and talk to him about nothing all that important. Any other day, I'd order him out of my house.

But right now, in this moment, I am happy to enjoy this and worry about the implications later.

17

QUINN

I should not be in this room.

Okay, I should, but the stirrups are making me uncomfortable. I waited out in the office for her to have the initial exam, but they are going to do a sonogram. I was happy to escape all the stares of the other people. Lord knows this is probably going to make that JSE thing Everly is always talking about. I was led down the hallway to the exam room.

"Hey, Quinn, you okay there, buddy?"

I look up from the metal contraptions. "Uh, yeah."

She giggles, the sound relaxing me. God, she has the best fucking giggles. I have a feeling she doesn't do it that often, or at least, not in front of a lot of people. It might be cliché, but when she giggles, it resonates with my soul. It's like if she's happy, I'm happy.

"You look like you're ready to pass out there."

"It's just," I swallow. "I hate doctor's offices and I don't know if I ever saw those things."

She glances down at the stirrups. "You'll probably get

used to seeing them."

I sigh and she giggles again.

The door opens and I blink at the woman standing there. Red hair, light green eyes, a massive smile. I know this girl. Wrong—woman.

"Piper?"

"Quinn Hawthorne. How the hell are you doing?"

She comes over to give me a hug.

"I didn't know you were the daddy."

"Uh, someone want to tell me what's going on here?" Everly asks, a note of irritation in her voice. I pull back from the hug to look over at her. She's looking like she wants to tear Piper's head off.

"Oh," Piper says stepping away. "We're old family friends."

"Yeah, remember the Abernathy Carter mentioned? That's her father." I look over at Carter's old playmate. "When did you move back here?"

"About three months ago."

"Well, I feel a little better about the stirrups now."

"Uh, okay," she says. There's another knock on the door and then a woman pops her head in. "Ready?"

"Yes, come on in. I want to see how big this baby is. Have a seat, Quinn."

I take the chair next to the exam table. I smile at Everly, who frowns at me. "Old family friends?"

"We did not date," Piper says with a laugh. "Although, I'm sure all the girls wanted to date all the brothers. Well, until Gavin came out. Nope. I take that back. I bet there were a few girls who would want to date Gavin just so they could stare at his beauty." She walks over and starts washing her hands. "But I left before dating. Boarding school."

She dries her hands, tossing the paper towels in the trash. "Now, let's look at this baby. From your chart, and what we discussed, you said you think you're about five weeks?"

Everly nods.

"Since you are that early, we'll need to do a transvaginal sonogram."

That does not sound good at all. What does she mean by transvaginal? Another wave of wooziness overcomes me. I don't feel like I'm going to be sick, but I do feel as if I might pass out.

Piper snaps her fingers. "You still with us, Quinn?"

I nod as Everly looks over at me.

"It just means I'll use a wand made for vaginas and not the huge one we usually use for the belly. Won't hurt Everly at all."

I release a breath.

"Were you really worried?" Everly asks, her gaze searching mine.

"Yeah. I mean, transvaginal does *not* sound good."

Everly smiles, then settles back against the cushioned exam table. It's at an incline. They drape a paper sheet over her knees as she settles them in the stirrups—still don't like them—and they start the sonogram.

"Hey, Denise, could you turn off the lights."

Once the lights are dimmed, she starts punching buttons on the machine.

"Okay, Mommy and Daddy," Piper says. My heart does skip a small beat at the sound of that. Not in a scared kind of way, but in a happy kind of way. "Let's check out this baby."

She takes her time, adjusting buttons.

"You said five weeks?"

"That's what I'm thinking."

She looks at me, then at Everly. "And before that?"

Everly looks at me. "Denver. So, what? Nine, ten weeks."

Ten weeks and three days.

Not that I'm counting or anything. I nod.

"Well, I think you are further along than you thought."

"What?" Everly asks, alarm turning her voice sharp.

"This baby is either growing at a rapid rate, or you are about two months along, not five weeks. When did you say you took the antibiotics?"

"Oh, shit, yeah, that was right before the Denver trip, not the trip to California." She looks at me. "Sorry."

"About what? Still my baby, right?"

She nods.

I take her hand. "That's all that matters."

She sighs, the sound filled with relief and I try not to get mad. She doesn't truly know me, so her reaction is probably considered normal.

"So, *this* is your baby," Piper says, breaking the moment. She's turned the monitor slightly so we can see the screen. "And you can see the heartbeat there."

"That looks insanely fast," Everly says.

"All normal. Babies have high heart rates at first, then they slow down the further along in the pregnancy we get."

I can't take my gaze from the screen. God, that little human is part me and part Everly. And...fuck, there's a lump in my throat.

"Alright there, Seven?" Everly asks.

I glance at her. "Yeah."

We share a smile, and all my worries from just a few minutes ago seem to fade away. Everly's rare smiles have the ability to do that.

"So, here's a picture of the baby."

She hands us a grainy black and white picture. We both look at it and I try to discern the image we saw on the screen. The nurse laughs.

"It's hard to figure out just where the baby is, sometimes." She points to a small speck in the middle. "There's the little sucker in the circle the doc made for you."

Everly and I both lean in closer to the picture. "Oh," we both say. When I look over at her, she's smiling but there is a sheen of tears. I know that Everly hates to show any emotion like that, but I can't help leaning closer and kissing her temple.

"Do you have any questions?" Piper says. I frown at her, but she's smiling at us.

"Uh, if I really am this far along, I had a glass or two of wine since then."

"Not to excess? And it was when?"

"Not too long after I got back from Denver."

She nods. "All should be good. Just avoid it from now on."

"I guess it's a good thing the smell of alcohol made me sick in San Diego."

Piper nods. "Makes sense. Pregnant women tend to have heightened senses, especially smell. Most doctors believe it's to protect the baby. Anything smells off, you aren't going to eat it. I'll have Denise get you some information about what you need to avoid other than that. You need to make sure you limit your caffeine, and there are a few foods to avoid."

"No coffee?"

"I would say no more than one a day."

Everly groans. "That sounds like torture."

"You'll be able to make it. I know that you own your own business, so make sure not to overdo anything."

"Oh, Becca won't allow me to do that."

Again, worry settles in my gut. I know they own the business together and I have nothing to do with it, but I want to be the person who makes sure she takes care of herself.

"No other questions then?"

We both shake our heads. "Okay, well, I'm going to want to see you in about four weeks, so when you stop by the reception desk, make sure to set up an appointment."

"Thanks, Dr. Abernathy," Everly says.

"Of course." She looks at me. "Say hi to your parents for me."

"Sure thing."

"I have those pamphlets in my office if you want to join me, Mr. Hawthorne," the nurse says.

I glance at Everly who nods. "I'll be out in the waiting room."

I squeeze her hand, then release it.

"Hey, Quinn? Can you put that pic in my purse?"

I don't want to give it up, but it will probably be safer in her purse.

I do as she requests, then I give her another kiss on her forehead. I follow the nurse out the door and down a hallway. She's yammering on about something, but I am not really connecting the words together. Seeing my baby...even if it doesn't look like a baby has me floating.

By the time we reach the nurses' desk area, I notice there are quite a few nurses and techs working.

"You didn't hear a word I said, did you?" the nurse asks me.

I force myself to look at her. It's not that it has anything to do with her, but my head is still spinning. My face flushes with embarrassment.

"Hey, don't worry. New daddies tend to be a little spacey. Just know that I've been doing this for fifteen years and I think Dr. Abernathy might be the best doctor I've worked with. Everly is in good hands."

"Thanks," I say, relief filtering through me. I assumed Piper was a good doc, mainly because she's always been whip smart just like her dad.

"Now, here are the pamphlets." She hands me a bunch of paper pamphlets. "You were fast."

She's looking over my shoulder at something and I turn to find Everly standing there. She looks exhausted and a little pale, but she's smiling.

"Let me make my appointment and then we can be out of here."

I nod, slipping my arm over her shoulders. I might not know what is going to happen to us, or with the baby, but I know that I have to be the luckiest man alive.

18

EVERLY

"So, Dr. Abernathy is a close family friend?" I ask Quinn as he backs out of the parking space at the clinic.

He glances over at me. "Yeah. She was Carter's playmate. They were thick as thieves when they were in elementary school."

That isn't enough information to satisfy me. "And after that?"

"Not sure. They grew apart the older they got as boys and girls do. Then she left for boarding school at around twelve? Yeah, I think it was twelve."

Again, I feel as if he is leaving out part of the story. I hate that I want to know, that there is a small part of me that wants to demand his history with Piper. I can't believe I'm jealous. Like really jealous of another woman. I don't think I've ever been jealous and I definitely don't like it.

"Everly?"

I blink and realize I've been staring down at my

hands, which are clenched on my lap. What the freak? I draw in a huge breath and calm myself.

"Rich people are weird."

"Why do you say that?"

"Why would you send your child off to school at that age? It's horrible. Especially for girls."

"Yeah, boys, they just want to be left alone."

"Oh, girls do too, but going through puberty and all that, much better with a mom around, I'm sure."

"I can see that," he remarks as he pulls into a parking slot just down the street from the diner. "Not that I know a lot about twelve-year-old girls."

"What? Don't tell me you weren't beating girls off with a stick."

His face flushes and he shrugs. "Not really. I was six feet tall by the time I was thirteen and kind of gangly. Also, I was a weirdo who liked to do art."

His ears are turning pink and it is the most adorable thing. Thinking of a thirteen-year-old Quinn full of awkwardness has my heart melting. "Try being a thirteen-year-old girl with a vocabulary that would make the devil blush and a big brother who scared the shit out of every male in middle school."

He smiles at me. "Well, either way, Hawthornes stick together. Although, I probably would have killed to go to boarding school if there was a good art program."

"My child will not go to boarding school."

He stares at me for a long moment, his gaze never wavering from my face. "*Our* child will not go to boarding school."

"Good, because, let's be honest. You could easily be a

complete asshole about this because you have more money."

"Well, I won't be, promise."

I believe him. One thing about Quinn is that he has a bone deep honesty he wears like a superhero cloak. I don't think he could lie if his life truly depended on it.

I look around at our surroundings and I realize he didn't ask me where to go after the appointment. "What are we doing here?"

"I thought you might be hungry."

Okay, I am hungry. After the queasiness, I always feel like I want to eat an entire cow. But that doesn't mean I have to like him figuring that out.

"And you just think this is where I want to eat? No discussion from me?" He doesn't say anything but his smile fades. "Quinn? Are you okay?"

He leans so close, I can feel his breath against my ear. "You know when you get all pissy like that, it gets me going, right? It makes me want to strip you out of those jeans and feast on your tasty pussy."

Oh, fuck, the man has a dirty mouth and I really like when he puts that mouth on me. My nipples are hard, my entire body is buzzing, and I am pretty sure I'll have to throw away my panties when we get back home.

"Every time you get snippy with me, think about that."

He's wearing a cocky smile when he pulls back from me. I want to be irritated—it's my favorite state of being —but I can't. He's so fucking sexy.

I don't say anything as I slip out of the car and regroup. I don't really have any playbook for this, and I need one. I don't operate well without it. I probably just need some more caffeine. I stop in my tracks and Quinn almost runs into me.

"What's wrong?"

I glance at him and realize he's really worried.

"I can't believe I have to give up coffee."

"Piper didn't say that. She said cut back."

I sigh and take a step in direction of the diner, but he puts his hand on my arm. "Hey, I didn't know when you wanted to tell people."

I shrug thinking about the issue. There will be no hiding it and part of me hates it but a bigger part really doesn't care. It's reality and everyone just needs to accept it. "People will find out soon enough because of your bionic sperm."

He chuckles, the sound of it coursing through my already tingly body. "How do you figure that my sperm are bionic?"

Feeling it's my turn to push him and get a little "Well, Mr. Hawthorne, we used condoms. Every time. Still got pregnant."

"I really like when you call me Mr. Hawthorne."

I laugh, unable to hold back how happy he does make me. Which should bother me because men have a tendency to use weaknesses against you, but I push those worries aside. "Well, if you play your cards right, I might call you that again."

I have my hand on the door handle when he stops me.

"Hey, I'm not going to push it right now. We're still trying to come to terms with all of this, but I wasn't sure how we planned to move forward. We'll need to talk about it at some point."

I nod but say nothing else as my phone starts to buzz in my pocket. I pull it out.

Becca: *So how did it go?*

Me: *Good. Apparently the Hawthornes know the new doc.*

Becca: *That's good, right?*

I don't respond because I know it is, but the jealousy I felt earlier has me pausing. I pick a booth by the window before answering.

Becca: *Isn't it?*

Me: *I guess.*

Becca: *Oh no. What happened?*

I could lie and say nothing, but this is Becca, the unicorn of friends who has the weird ability to know there is something bothering me. She will be relentless. I'm still amazed I hid Quinn for so long.

Me: *I got jealous. She's gorgeous.*

Becca: *So are you.*

Me: *You love me. You have to say that.*

Becca: *NOT TRUE. If I liked ladies I would so do you. Do you hard.*

Becca: *Where are you now?*

Me: *At the diner.*

Becca: Y*ou need me? Freddy's here and it's slow.*

"Do you mind if Becca joins us for lunch?"

"Not at all."

Me: *Sure.*

Becca: *Wyatt's here. Been here all morning. And he just invited himself.*

Me: *Why is he still there.*

"Crap. Sorry, my brother was there. He invited himself."

"Mason?"

That makes me chuckle. Wyatt is a hard ass, and Quinn will have to learn to deal with him. "Nope, sorry. That other idiot."

Becca: *Carter was very flirty with me, even though he is always like that with just about everyone. Wyatt lost his shit over it and was being all big brother.*

That is not what was happening there, but she will never believe me if I told her he was jealous.

"And apparently your brother didn't give a good first impression."

"So, Carter pissed him off?"

I laugh. "How did you know it was Carter?"

"You've met him. Now compare him to Grady and think about it."

I nod. "Okay, that makes sense."

We order our drinks — water for me because of the alien in my belly—and coffee for Quinn.

"You could have decaf," Quinn says when I frown at him after he gives the order.

"What is the point of that?"

He smiles at me and dammit, I find myself softening even more. Then he rises and comes to my side of the booth.

"What are you doing?"

"I'm not sitting next to your brother."

I scoot over because I understand. We're still looking over the menus when the bell over the door rings. Becca looks like a very angry Barbie as she stomps down the aisle with an equally irritated Wyatt.

"Hi, Everly. Quinn," Becca says as she stands by the end of the table.

"Is everything okay?" Quinn asks.

I know what's wrong with her. "You can get a hug later, Becca."

She sighs and slips into the booth. Wyatt nods to both of us, then settles in beside her.

"How did the appointment go?" Wyatt asks.

"Fine."

Quinn is looking between Wyatt and me. He knows I'm doing this on purpose to be an ass, so he takes pity on my brother.

"I know the doctor."

"You do?" Wyatt asks.

Quinn nods. "Old family friend. She grew up with Carter."

"Small world," Wyatt murmurs.

"Right? I mean, she gave Everly a transvaginal sonogram and I used to have to babysit her."

"What the fuck is that?" Of course that comes from Wyatt.

"I had that same reaction to the name. But it was nothing really."

"It's not like you had something stuck up your vagina," I say, dark humor lacing my words.

"First, I don't have a vagina. Second, we got to see the heartbeat and Piper gave us a picture of the baby."

"A picture of the..." Becca looks around.

"Oh, who cares, Becca. Everyone is going to find out. And sooner rather than later."

"What's that mean?"

"I'm either going to birth a giant, which would make sense considering how big Quinn is, or I'm closer to three months along." I pull out the grainy pic. Becca reaches across the table and grabs it out of her hand so quickly I blink.

"Oh...this doesn't..." she looks up.

Quinn leans forward. "Doesn't look like much right now, but see the circle on there?"

She nods.

"That's the baby."

"A baby?"

We turn and look at the waitress who is looking at all of us with rapt attention. Of course we had to have Rhonda for our waitress today. She's got the biggest mouth and she hates me just because I broke her nose when we were in the sixth grade.

Well, I guess it's a good thing I hadn't planned on keeping this a secret.

19

QUINN

The meal goes off without a hitch, mainly because Wyatt keeps tossing nasty looks at Becca. I don't know what happened with Carter, but it must have had to do with Becca.

"I was thinking we could go to San Antonio for dinner tonight," I say as casually as I can. From the look on Everly's face, I did not accomplish my mission. The thing about Everly is that she notices every damn thing.

"You want me to meet your parents?"

I smile. "I thought they should meet you before the birth."

"What will you do when your career takes a dive?" Wyatt grumbles at me.

Most people would probably be pissed at the comment, but he helped raise Everly. He's looking out for her and our baby.

"I will kick you out of this booth," Becca says. He ignores her and from the dangerous look she's giving him, he's doing it at his own peril.

"I don't mind, Becca. And I guess you don't pay attention to much about Syd, but she works for my family."

He nods. "The At Home Network."

"Well, that and all the clubs that Carter is opening, and a few other things."

"What does that have to do with you?"

"I'm on the board. Not that I have much to offer, but I am a voting member."

"And?"

Jesus, this guy. I mean, I get it. He loves his sister and I'm okay with showing him just how much I'm worth, but I have never really cared about all that. The only thing I like about it is that it gives me the ability to be a writer and artist.

"He's trying not to say that he's probably considered a millionaire," Everly says as she continues to eat.

Wyatt studies me for a long moment, then nods and gets back to eating.

"Are you working on the next book?" Becca asks me.

I nod. "Always."

She smiles. "My mom's the same way. She's an artist and not, you know, *the* Q. Hawthorne, but she's always thinking about her art. She's always been like that. Are you going to be done soon?"

"I planned on being done sooner, but the book decided to go another way."

"Another way?" That question comes from Everly.

I turn to look at her and nod. "New character."

I should probably get her permission before I write the whole book with her in it, but I figured it would be best that she sees the whole thing at first. If she says no, I'll just have to come up with something else.

I nod. "Sort of wreaked havoc on my timeline in the book so I'm reworking it."

"Hmm," is all she says, but I'm happy that she's eating. She is normally slim, but I'm sure the recent weight loss is because of the morning sickness.

"So, San Antonio?"

"To meet your parents?"

I nod. "And I'm sure Gavin would like to meet you, but I can tell him to fuck off if you want to wait."

Her mouth twitches. "I'm okay with him being there. I'm just not sure about the eating."

I let loose a breath I didn't know I was holding in. I'm not nervous about what my parents will think of Everly. I have a feeling my mom will love her to pieces. I make a mental note to warn my mom.

Me: *Hey, are you guys back in town?*
Mom: *We'll be back tonight.*
Me: *Okay. I wanted to bring a friend to dinner.*
Mom: *Is this of the female variety friend?*
Me: *Yes.*
Mom: *Fantastic. More estrogen to fight the sausagefest I deal with every day.*

Yeah, that's my mom.

"So?"

I smile at her. "Not tonight. Tomorrow. Mom and Dad were in New York with Gavin and Oliver."

"Gavin is Grady's twin, right?"

I nod. "Fraternal, so not identical."

"He is just as gorgeous," Becca says. Wyatt frowns at

her. Truthfully, he frowns all the time. I'm not sure what I would do if he smiled.

"Oliver's his husband. And my agent."

"Oh, I thought your whole family lived here."

"For the most part. I think Oliver is working with his partners to move down here. No reason to live in New York after they adopt the baby. Oliver's entire family lives in Texas and Louisiana. I normally split time between New York and San Antonio, but I've mostly been in Texas over the last few months."

She nods and asks me nothing else, but the fact that she's asking questions is probably a good sign.

"Since you didn't get to see much yesterday, you should come by the store and look around," Becca says.

"Sounds good."

I insist on paying for breakfast, which upsets Wyatt and Everly. That family seems to have a hard head and chip on their shoulder trait. Hopefully, it won't be too strong in our child.

The moment we step into Nerdvana, I get that same feeling as I did yesterday. Explosions of color, although orderly, draws me in a lot of directions. But, of course, I'm a self-centered artist so I walk over to the display with Danvers.

"I got him from your publisher."

I glance over at her. "I didn't even know they did this."

"You don't do signings or appearances. Why is that? I thought that people like you wanted to do those things."

"I don't."

"Why?"

I smile. Leave it to Everly to be blunt. Most people—other than Oliver—dance around why I won't go.

"I like meeting the regular fans, and all the people who work in the stores. Y'all are the reason I have a fan base. But the super fans…they scare me. I had a woman stalk me from a comic convention all the way back here to Texas. She showed up outside my parents' house."

"Jesus."

"And that's why I stopped."

"Makes sense. Come on, I'll show you around."

She's holding out her hand and I know this is a big deal. Granted, I have touched—and licked—almost every inch of her body. I've heard her moan out my name and felt her come on my cock. But this is intimate, normal. Not really sexual at all but just as much of a turn on.

And right now, that is more important to me than anything else. This connection is strong. I just have to convince her of it.

WE GET HOME IN THE EARLY AFTERNOON AND WE SHARE A quiet meal together for dinner. After I clean up—which she argues about, but I ignore her—we snuggle on the couch and she ends up with her head on my lap snoring softly through Tony Stark's lines and I smile. I slip out from beneath her, then pull her up off the couch.

Once I have her in her bed, I decide to make her a little more comfortable. I know from my experience with her, and what she's told me, she mostly sleeps naked. So, I pull off her sweats and top, she'd gotten rid of the bra the moment we came in the house, and then tuck her under the covers. I leave her there as I go brush my teeth, then I take off my clothes, my body and mind exhausted from the day. I join her in bed and because it's just a full-sized bed, we are snuggled up next to each other. While I don't mind the snuggling, I definitely need to have my California king moved up here. My feet go right to the edge of the mattress.

I settle in behind her, my cock hard against her ass. I probably won't get any sleep in this condition but right now Everly needs her sleep. But she pushes her ass back against me, and I groan. The giggle makes me smile. I rise up, pulling her back so she's laying face up on the mattress.

"What the hell?" I say, trying to give her a frown, but I have a feeling because she smiles up at me. She slides her fingers over my cheek.

"Something wrong, Seven?"

The nickname never fails to send rush of heat blazing through me. "Yeah. You were deliberately trying to get me hard."

"First, you came to bed hard. Second, why is that a bad thing?"

I blink. "We didn't discuss...you know."

She snorts. "God, you're adorable. You can say the word sex, and why would it be a problem now?"

I open my mouth to tell her, but then snap it shut. It's then that I realize this is much more than the crush I thought I had on her. I knew I was getting attached to her, but I didn't understand my true feelings.

I'm falling in love with her.

This is bad. Yes, we're having a baby and we will be in each other's lives for eternity because of that. But right now, I can't think of another woman I want, who understands my needs all the while making sure she's her own person.

How could I not fall in love with her?

"You have a strange look on your face."

My gaze finally focuses on her worried expression. If I tell her know, she'll freak. Her knee jerk reaction will be to toss me out of her house and that won't do. No, it would be better to devise a plan to make her fall in love with me, and to do that, I need to stay close to her.

"Contemplating my revenge."

"Oh," her eyebrows shoot up to her hairline. "And what have you come up with?"

The teasing note in her voice has my cock twitching. This woman. From the moment I met her, I've been twisted up with her. And now…she's even sexier.

"Well…" I slip down her body, pulling her panties off easily. I can already smell her desire.

"You think this is torture?"

"I think if I don't let you come, it is torture."

"You wouldn't do that."

She's right, I wouldn't. But I can pretend. Instead of lying, I just dip my head between her legs and find her damp, her need coating her inner lips. I slip my tongue inside of her, enjoying the taste of her, then move to her clit, taking it between my teeth as I thrust two fingers deep inside her. She shivers and moans.

I then rise to my knees, taking her along with me, slipping my hands beneath her ass and feasting on her pussy. It doesn't take long to get her up to the edge. I pause and look down at her. I want her to know who exactly is giving her pleasure, to acknowledge it.

"Everly."

Her eyes flutter open. As she watches, I lick her slit, from the bottom all the way up to her clit. She shivers in response, but I only tease her. I don't let her fall over into pleasure just yet. No, her sweet pussy is going to be wrapped around me when she comes.

Then something else hits me.

"Fuck, need my wallet."

I go to look for it, but she stops me.

"Quinn, just fuck me. You're clean, I'm pregnant, who cares. Just. Fuck. Me."

"If you insist," I say, pushing my knit boxers down far enough to grab hold of my cock. I enter her fast and hard and, fuck, it feels good. I've never had sex raw. I can feel every little ripple of her inner muscles and it is the most amazing thing.

I move then, pushing deeper inside of her. I take my time still, pushing her along to the pinnacle, but also, showing how much I care for her. With every kiss, every caress, I try to let her know just how I feel without saying the words that I know will freak her out. Soon, though, she's close and I can't wait to see her come. I slip my hand between our bodies as I thrust deeper inside of her.

"Quinn," she screams, as she bows up off the bed. I lean down and take a nipple into my mouth, sucking hard as I continue to thrust in and out of her.

She wraps her legs around my waist, which allows me to thrust into her at a deeper angle. Soon, I'm coming, pouring myself into her, losing myself in the feel of her pussy clinging to my cock.

I'm drained, but instead of collapsing on her, I pull out of her, then settle on the mattress, pulling her into my arms.

"I think we both won that battle," I murmur, chuckling.

"Yeah, and that's the best way."

She snuggles in closer. A few moments later her steady breathing tells me that she's drifted off to sleep. I follow her, knowing that it is just a small battle in the war to win her heart, but I'm up for the challenge.

20

THE HAWTHORNE BROTHER TEXT THREAD

Quinn: *What the fuck did you do to Wyatt, Carter?*
Carter: *Absolutely nothing.*
Grady: *He was overly flirty with Becca.*
Carter: *#lies*
Gavin: *Should I know anything about any of these people?*
Carter: *No. Go be happy with your hubby.*
Gavin: *Now I have to know.*
Carter: *Everly—the girl he hooked up with in Denver— lives in Juniper Springs and is now his Baby Mama.*
Quinn: *Carter!*
Carter: *Also, she owns that little comic book shop I've been raving about with her friend Becca who is the sweetest.*
Grady: *You met her the morning we had to bail out Sydney.*
Sydney: *Why am I even in this discussion?*
Grady: *Sorry, love, but you're stuck with all of them now. You're part of the family.*
Carter: **gif-one-of-us**
Oliver: *What the actual hell is happening down in Texas?*
Quinn: *Better you don't know right now.*

Oliver: *Is this the woman you slept with before you started writing and drawing again?*
Carter: *It is.*
Oliver: *Then everyone needs to leave the artist alone.*
Quinn: *Thank you.*
Carter: *You started this thread, Captain America.*
Quinn: **middle finger emoji**
Gavin: *Wait. Did Carter say you have a baby mama?*
Quinn: *Yes.*
Gavin: *And you didn't tell me?*
Quinn: *Sorry. Just found out and I was going to be in San Antonio tomorrow. I was going to tell you and folks in person. Carter ruined it. Don't tell Mom and Dad.*
Carter: **you're-welcome-jack-sparrow-gif**
Quinn: *Funny story. Piper Abernathy is her doctor.*
Grady: *Piper? God, I haven't seen her in years.*
Gavin: *She was always such a sweet girl.*
Oliver: *Why are we talking about this when Quinn could be working?*
Grady: *What happened between you two, Carter? Piper and you used to spend all your time together when you were little.*

A few minutes later:

Grady: *Carter?*

21

EVERLY

I wake up slowly the next morning, blinking against how light my room is. I usually wake up much earlier thanks to Bert and Ernie. I look over at the clock. It's already nine o'clock.

Dammit. I overslept. I sit up and the first thing I notice is I'm naked. I sleep naked sometimes, but since I started waking up sick, I've made sure to at least have a t-shirt on.

Then last night comes rushing back to me. Quinn taking care of me, being so sweet, then ...GAWD. He made love to me. It was fast and at times hard, but there was a thread of sweetness to it that makes me all gooey inside.

Speaking of which, where the hell is he? He left his t-shirt on the chair in the corner of my room, so I grab it, slipping it on. For some reason, I'm not feeling that bad this morning, so that's something. I also get a fresh pair of panties and put them on before heading to the bathroom. After taking care of business, and happy again that I'm not throwing up my insides, I look for my phone. I frown when it's not sitting on my bedside table. And yes, I know that's a bad idea, but I need it for the time. I wake up at all hours during the night, although I didn't last night, so maybe I left it out in the living room.

I go in search of it and instead find Quinn.

He's sitting in my kitchen drawing. I have a feeling that's something he does all the time. The short times we've been together—the second and third time at least—he drew a lot.

I lean against the door jamb and watch him. Again, he's so damned sexy when he draws. He's sitting there in a pair sleep pants and nothing else. His hair is a mess from sleep, and I like to think my hands.

"You going to stand there and watch me all day?"

"Maybe," I respond, walking forward.

He pushes back from the table and pulls me into his lap.

"Good morning, Everly."

"Good morning, Quinn."

"How are you feeling?"

"Pleasant for the first time in a long time."

"Good. I don't like the idea of you being sick."

"You and me, babe." I glance at the drawing and laugh. It's Bert and Ernie with their mouths open as torn bread pieces rain down on them.

"I'm surprised they didn't bother me this morning."

"I took care of them."

"Thanks."

"They are assholes though, aren't they? They would not leave without some bread."

I nod laughing. "Yeah."

"And they've never had a female around?"

I shake my head. "One or two have tried to venture closer to them, but they run all of them off."

"They picked the one place in Texas that is truly perfect for them, then." He's studying me like he's worried about something.

"What?"

"Becca texted me this morning."

I try to get up out of his lap, but he holds onto me.

"Nope. You are not going in."

"I have a business to run."

"No. Becca said, and I quote, 'I will call Mama if she comes in before she feels well enough today.'"

"Ugh. Mrs. Gold is tough."

"So," he says. "I'm going to make some coffee, and I figure you might just want to have some bone broth?"

The mention of food makes my stomach gurgle. I jump up off his lap and, this time he must see something in my expression because he lets me go. I run as fast as I can to the bathroom. I'm hacking up the lining of my stomach when I feel cool hands pull my hair back. I should be embarrassed, but seriously, the stomach lining is not an easy thing to throw up.

By the time I'm done, I sit back, and he lets go of my hair. He then grabs a washrag and wets it down, wringing it out before he presses it against my forehead. Oh, god, that feels fantastic.

"Thank you," I say.

"Sure thing."

Then he sits down on the floor with me. I glance over at him as I hold the rag against my hot face.

"I should be embarrassed."

"I think you shouldn't be, although I understand it. So glad Carter isn't here though."

"Why?"

"He has a gag reflex. He hears someone throwing up, he loses it."

"Nice to know." I sigh. "I'm still embarrassed."

He frowns as he takes my free hand in his. "How about I tell you something really embarrassing so we're even?"

"Okay."

"Let's see...oh, I have one."

"Lay it on me."

"You know I've had issues with fans."

I nod and lean closer so I can lay my head on his shoulder, as if it is the most normal thing in the world.

"I had one contact my mother and tell her we had just gotten married."

"Are you sure there was no Las Vegas wedding?" I tease.

He chuckles, that low sexy sound that I would hear in my dreams. There is just something so solid about him.

"I am positive. I was away on my honeymoon."

Just hearing the fact that he had been married once has my stomach dipping. I swallow, fighting against the nausea. I've never been the kind of woman who judged her partners on their past sexual lives. Most of the time, I didn't even know—or care—what they did before they met me. Or after. But Quinn is different. I could say it's because the alien inside of me, but I've felt it since we hooked up in Denver.

"How did she know your parents?"

"She didn't, but they were easy to get to. Also, not many people didn't know I got married. We had kept it kind of low key."

I remember. I had never seen him, but when I heard Q. Hawthorne had married, my heart had broken just a little bit. It was stupid, but I felt as if he had abandoned me.

"Did she have mental issues?"

"No. I've had my share of people like that, but this one, she was trying to get money out of my parents."

"What a skank."

"Exactly. The best part about all of it is that she went into massive detail about our 'sex life'." He uses air quotes around sex life

"That's not embarrassing because it isn't true."

"It is when your brother decides to read the email at the first family dinner after your honeymoon."

"Oh, no."

"Yeah, and he added more adjectives and descriptions—not to mention the sounds he used."

I can't fight the laugh. That man is insane. "I have no idea how Carter survived."

"How did you know it was Carter?"

I raise my head and look at him with one of my eyebrows raised. He laughs.

"Okay, yeah, the rest of us wouldn't do it. The truth was, he was nineteen and hated my ex. He thought it might break us up."

I digest that bit of information and realize I want to know what actually did break them up. That little tidbit of information gets under my skin. I don't do long term. Well, I didn't.

"You want to know why we broke up."

Not a question, and that scares me. This man knows me better than everyone except maybe Becca. I lay my head down on his shoulder once more. I shouldn't want to know, but...

"Yeah. I kind of do want to know."

"Couple of things. She wanted to live the party life. She liked crowds and the attention."

"Talk about a skank."

I hear the smile in his voice when he speaks next. "And she wanted to put off having kids."

I raise my head once more, my gaze colliding with his. "You wanted kids before this?"

"Of course."

"There is no *of course* about it. I never thought I would have kids because I am never getting married."

Everything in him seems to still, as if he isn't even breathing and he's one of those wax figures.

"Never getting married?"

I shake my head. "I...let's just say that I never wanted to. Not really."

And I'm lying again. I wanted to at one time. But that had been before Trent, before college, before everything. I'm so cynical I don't think I'll ever get past the idea that there is a happily ever after. Relationships don't really last, but in a few cases. I don't think it's worth the pain a failed relationship would cost me.

"Hmm," is all he says before he kisses my forehead. "I'm going to heat up some of that bone broth from your brother. Will you be okay?"

I smile at him and nod. "Thank you."

"Is it always that bad?"

"No. It was much worse before now."

"Before now?"

"Before I had someone here to help me."

He blinks, then his lips curve into that sexy smile that makes my nipples so hard there's a good chance they could cut through glass. He gives me another kiss on the forehead, then stands before helping me up.

Once I'm alone, I look at myself in the mirror. I look a little better than I did yesterday. I have more color and I don't look like death warmed over.

I think back to Quinn's last comment about marriage, or rather non comment. He didn't seem particularly upset with the idea of not marrying, and that should make me happy, right? I mean, that's what I want.

Then why do I have a hollow pit in the bottom of my stomach? It's insane.

With a sigh, I grab my toothbrush and toothpaste. Thinking about silly things like that is a waste of time. Maybe it's just the hormones. Whatever the reason, I concentrate on brushing my teeth. By the time I'm done, I have pushed it out of my brain, mostly.

As I'm walking down the hall, I hear my phone vibrating and see it on the table I keep in the hallway for keys and everything else.

Becca: *Quinn said you were up and about but sick.*
Me: *Lies.*

Becca: *Don't even try that crap with me.*
I think they're conspiring against me.
Me: *I did but I feel better.*
Becca: *You need to eat. Did you eat?*
Me: *Quinn's heating up some broth.*
Becca: *Good. That's really sweet.*

I don't respond right away because I know she's building up some kind of fantasy where we fall in love and live happily ever after. Worse, there is a tiny part of me that would like to indulge in that fantasy. But I can't. Life isn't a fantasy.

Me: *More like he feels guilty.*

That's a lie and she probably knows it. She takes pity on me and doesn't remark on that.

Becca: *When you can for sure say you will not Linda Blair all over our store, you can come in.*
Me: *#Rude*
Becca: *#truestory*
Becca: *On both accounts.*

I smile as I set my phone down before it's vibrating again. I see texts from my brothers in a group chat, but the phone is taken out of my hands by Quinn.

"Hey," I say, frowning at him.

He shakes his head. "You need to eat."

I glance past him and see the bowl of soup sitting on the table.

"Fine."

I stomp over and sit down.

"And thanks for heating this up."

"You're welcome. Do you want your coffee now or do you want to wait?"

I know what he's talking about. I get one cup and I need to make sure I take advantage of it.

"Let me try some water, first."

He smiles at me as he joins me at the table. I normally hate being taken care of. It makes me feel weak, but with Quinn, it doesn't for some reason. Instead, I just feel... content. Which is an odd feeling for me.

"What is going on in there?" He asks, pointing to my head. I blink and look at him. He's now wearing an old-faded t-shirt that clings to his big arms and the sleep pants. They are made out of some kind of knit material that doesn't hide anything...if you get my drift. But his first instinct is to take care of me. Normally, I would hate that from a guy, but from Quinn, it just feels natural and that has me nervous.

"Nothing."

He chuckles, the sound of it leaving me a little breathless. I hide it by sipping my soup.

"I highly doubt that, Everly Spencer."

"Why?"

"Your brain probably is always working on something, which I find sexy as fuck."

I blink again. This man always says things like that to me, and I kind of like it.

He sips his coffee while I eat, and I find the quiet between us pleasant. When I'm with other people, they always seem to want to fill in the quiet moments. Sometimes, I need the air around me to be silent. From our time together, I realize Quinn is the same as me.

"Why don't you want to get married?"

That is until he throws out things like that.

"I haven't had a good experience with relationships."

"So, you've had them."

I nod.

"And?"

I sigh. "I had my first and only serious relationship in college."

"Until now."

That stops me. I study the way his cheek is flexing, which tells me he's grinding his teeth. "What?"

"You're in a serious relationship with me."

My first instinct is to push back, but I see the determined glint in his green gaze. I nod.

He relaxes so I continue.

"Then, Trent the Asshole happened."

"Trent?"

"I dated in high school, even slept with a guy or two, but he was my first real experience with a relationship. You know, when you stay at each other's houses, actually sleep together."

"Yeah."

"And in the end, I found out that it wasn't that he liked me, it was that I filled a box."

"I don't understand."

He wouldn't, mainly because he's a good man. "I had a few of my tats by then. I filled the box of sleeping with a woman with tattoos. As soon as I had sex with him, he dumped me. Then I found out about the contest he and his stupid frat brothers were having."

"What the actual fuck?"

"And from that point on, I decided it wasn't worth it."

He studies me for a second, then says, "You didn't deserve that."

Just that simple statement has a lump rising in my throat. I blink back tears and nod. I've never really told anyone but Becca, and his easy acceptance of my side of the story says so much about the man.

"That's the reason? It has nothing to do with me?"

My eyes widen. "No."

"Good to know."

Then it's quiet again, both of us sitting in an easy silence that doesn't seem to bother either one of us.

"I texted with Mom and I think we'll wait a couple days before we head down."

"Oh?"

"Yeah. I think we need to get your morning sickness under control. Plus, it will be easier for everyone to be there on the weekend."

I nod. My phone goes off again and he chuckles.

"I take it this is Becca's mom?"

Mama Gold: *You will bring the man to my house so I can check him out or I will show up at your house today.*

Mama Gold: *Dinner is at six.*

"Welcome to Juniper," I say, sarcasm heavy in my tone.

The smile he gives me is brilliant.

"I think I'm gonna like it here."

22

QUINN

I glance over at Everly as I turn onto my parents' street. They live in the same house they raised us in. I remember moving there when I was about six or so. And I guess from someone on the outside, it looks like a big house. I mean, it *is* a big house, but it's always just been home to us.

Everly is picking at her jeans, and I can almost hear her inner thoughts as she works through everything she argued before we left. I know if she were being rational, Everly would be cool with this meeting. However, from what little she told me, she has never been the kind of woman who met the parents.

I park my car and notice only Gavin is here. That's good at least.

She draws in a breath and releases it.

"They're going to love you."

She gives me a look that tells me she doesn't believe me.

"Yeah, billionaires are usually really happy about their sons knocking up a woman like me."

"First of all, my mother is going to adore the woman you are. Secondly, if they don't like it, they can fuck off."

She blinks.

"That's right. No matter where we go or what happens to us, we will be connected, and that's more important than anything in the world."

She continues to stare at me, her gaze moving back and forth between my eyes. She opens her mouth to respond, but there's a loud knock on the driver's side window and, from her expression—it's one my mother has worn more than once—I know who it is.

I open the door, stepping out, and before I can do anything else, Carter hugs me.

"I missed you, buddy."

I sigh, patting him on the back. "I saw you three days ago, Carter."

"Still." Then he abandons me and hurries over to hug Everly. The look of panic on her face almost makes me laugh, but I hold it back. Mainly because she is going to have to get used to Carter and his affection. He's like a massive golden retriever who has a sweet tooth for anything that involves ice cream.

He pulls back. "You look better."

"Thank you, I guess?" She looks at me and I decide she's had enough of Carter. She is going to have to deal with my mother as soon as she finds out about the pregnancy.

"That's enough, Carter," I say, pushing him aside.

Once I have hold of Everly, I turn to Carter. "Do not reveal the news. I want to do it myself."

"Fine." The tone in his voice tells me that he isn't happy.

As we turn to go inside, Sydney and Grady show up. Syd looks a little frazzled as she slips out of the car and hurries over to Everly. Another hug. Another look of panic.

"How are you doing?" Syd asks.

"Okay." No one picks up on the nerves, but I do. I can hear it in the sharpness of her tone and the way her body language tells me she would rather be anywhere else.

"Just so you know, Quinn wants to tell Mom and Dad," Carter announces it as if that would be a surprise. I sigh and Syd gives me a nod telling me she'll control him. She seems to be the one other person who can put him in his place, other than my mother. We all start walking toward the front door, Syd and Grady leading the way with Carter close behind them.

"Don't say anything to your father about his eyebrows," Syd tosses back over her shoulder.

"Did he blow himself up again?"

"Yep, although we're all pretending it didn't happen," Grady says as he holds the door open for Syd, and Carter steps forward to follow her. Grady pushes him out of the way and lets the door shut in his face.

Everly snorts.

"What's that about?" she asks, quietly.

"Dad tends to blow himself up about once a year with the gas grill."

She's staring up at me, so I lean forward and brush my mouth over her cheek.

"What was that for?" she asks, suspicion filling her voice.

"Just in case you were nervous."

"Well, I'm not." I stop and raise one eyebrow and she laughs. "Okay, I am a little."

I squeeze her hand. "I understand. Mr. Gold is much scarier than my father."

I met Becca's parents the day before when Becca had insisted on hosting a dinner at her house. It had gone okay until she and Wyatt got into another fight over something trivial. It was so trivial, I can't even remember what the fight was about, but the one thing I remember from the meal was Jason Gold giving me a stare down, then telling me if Everly is hurt, he has a lot of land to disappear a body. Becca is apparently a lot like her stepfather.

"Okay. But Mr. Jason is a sweetie."

I snort but make no other comments. We step into the house and I can hear voices in the living room. I peek in and see that Gavin and Grady are at the bar, Carter is telling them they don't know how to mix drinks, so it's a normal day for the Hawthorne brothers.

"Mom is probably in the dining room."

As we walked down the hall, I see Everly peeking at the framed pictures on the walls. For all the money my parents have, their house looks more middle class. They both grew up in working class families, so they have never really been comfortable being billionaires.

Granted, they travel by private jets, and Dad retired early, but I'm proud of the fact that they are normal.

We stop at the doorway and I look at her. For the first time, I see beneath the nerves and it makes my heart ache. I want to beat the shit out of Trent the Asshole. I would hunt him down if I thought it would make her believe in herself, and as much as she says that it doesn't bother her anymore, it has shaped her romantic relationships for over a decade.

"Ready?"

She licks her lips and nods. I lean closer to brush my mouth over hers and, of course, I can't control myself. Neither of us is very good at the whole control thing. I cup her face and deepen the kiss.

"Good god, give the woman some breathing space, Quinn," my mother says.

Everly pulls back and mutters 'unfuckingbelievable' under her breath.

"I heard that," I say with a smile. "Come on, she's going to love you."

23

EVERLY

Ellen Hawthorne is not what I expected. I know what Quinn said, but still, she is...normal. I thought rich people acted weird, like bought tigers and things like that. Ellen is not like that.

I glance at Quinn as she goes on and on about my tats.

"This one is gorgeous. Who is she?" Ellen asks as she points to my Becca tattoo. I have a small figure of her dressed up in her favorite unicorn outfit. We're sitting in the dining room with Syd and Ellen as Quinn's father gives instructions to the cook. That is one rich person thing, though, they have a cook.

"That's my bestie, Becca."

"I told you that she and Becca own that shop Nerdvana," Syd says. "I know I've mentioned the store before."

"Oh, yes," she says with a smile showing me her one dimple. "So amazing that you're blazing your own trail. I'm going to have to make a trip up there. Also, I have to see this Wyatt's place." She turns to Syd. "Are you allowed back in yet?"

I smile at the question. When Syd and Grady hit hard times, she had shown up in the bar and started a fight. Wyatt had banned Syd and Nancy—her bestie— for six months.

"I told you before that I was," Syd says with a laugh. I blink. I thought someone like Ellen would be upset by it. "And another connection: Wyatt is Everly's brother."

"Ah, all the little connections in small towns. I grew up in one too, so I know what that's like."

Just then, Quinn's father Peter strides into the dining room. If Ellen and Quinn share a smile, Peter and Quinn share their height and easy-going style. He's like an older copy of what all of the men in the family will probably look like when they get older. Well, except for the missing eyebrows.

"I got banned from my own outdoor kitchen."

"You shouldn't blow yourself up and that wouldn't happen. This is Everly Spencer. She's the person Carter and Quinn were talking about a few weeks ago."

It's then that he notices us. It's like Ellen was the only person in the world to him when he came into the room. He smiles at me and, geez, I realize that Carter is almost a carbon copy of his father. He comes over and, again, I'm besieged with a hug. This family. I mean, my family is nice, and my idiot brothers would hug me more if I was okay with it. But, these people, they just ignore that and hug you.

He pulls back. "It is very nice to meet you. Took him long enough to bring you."

Quinn could have thrown me under the bus, but instead he says, "I was busy with the book."

His father nods. "So, I hear you own a store."

I nod.

"We'll go over all that later," Ellen says. Her gaze settles on me. "I have a feeling they have something to tell us."

"Did Carter tell you something?" Quinn asks, suspicion threading his tone.

Ellen smiles and shakes her head. "No, but he's been avoiding me, which means he has news he's afraid he'll tell me. Let's sit down."

After we take our seats, I realize how nervous I am. My palms are damp, and my head is spinning. That might have more to do with the fact that I haven't eaten since about nine this morning and that was just some bone broth. Again. That is getting really old.

"Everly's pregnant."

There is a beat of silence, then his mother screams. She pops up out of her chair and comes over. She ignores Quinn and pulls me out of my chair and hugs me. For a second, I don't react, because it's kind of over the top for me. Then, my eyes burn. I slip my arms around her. I now understand why Quinn is so damned affectionate. His entire family are some of the warmest people I have ever met, other than the Golds.

"Well, that's fantastic," his father says behind us. "I like two cousins growing up together."

I pull back and look at his father.

"Gavin and Oliver are adopting. So, there will be two cousins to grow up together. That's good."

I smile at his brother and husband. No one looks upset, although most of the family knows now. Well, everyone knew before we showed up. And apparently, at that moment, Ellen realizes her reaction is different than everyone else's.

"Did everyone else know about this?" Irritation is easy to hear in her voice.

None of the brothers say anything, but they are all looking anywhere but at their mother.

"Boys!"

All four men look at her. "I want answers."

Pete comes up and pulls her into his arms. Seeing the love between the two of them is kind of sweet. It reminds me of Becca's mother and stepfather.

"Now, Ellen, let's just concentrate on what we found out. We're going to have another grandbaby."

She sighs. "Okay, but you four are in the doghouse. No cookies for any of you." She turns her attention to me, her smile as welcoming as before we told her about the baby. "Why don't you boys go away?"

She isn't even being subtle. I chuckle and look at Quinn, who doesn't look like he wants to leave me.

"Go. I'm sure your mother isn't going to eat me."

He leans in and gives me a kiss. "Call if you need me."

As soon as he leaves, she rolls her eyes. "So sweet, that boy. I've never seen him act like that around other women. Even, you know, *that* woman." She waves her hands dismissing the subject that she just brought up. "Never mind about that. Let's sit down and you can tell me all about Nerdvana and your bestie. Have a seat and I'll be right back."

She's only gone a minute, but Syd says, "Don't worry. She loves you."

"How can you tell?"

"You make Quinn happy. That's all that matters to them."

Ellen reappears with a glass of water and some crackers. She sets them in front of me. "I know what you are going through. Just let me know if there is anything else I can get for you."

I smile, my nerves and my stomach settling a little bit. "Sure."

"So, what's it like running your own store?"

"You've been quiet since we left my parents' house," Quinn remarks as we walk into my house.

"Just tired." It's a lie. I mean, I am tired, but that's not why I'm quiet. I just keep thinking over all the things that his mother said. She likes me because I make her son happy. What happens when that stops? Because this is me, and I screw things up. I don't know how to open myself up to another person. And I can see that I will hurt him at some point. It's what I do.

"There's something wrong. Did Mom say something to upset you?"

"No."

"Then what."

I sigh. I'm so tired and I just want to curl into a ball and sleep for five days. I know it's a mistake, but all the little worries have been driving me crazy. Now seeing how normal his family is, I can't understand his attraction.

"Why are you here, Quinn? What's the real reason you're sticking around?"

He lets a beat of silence go by before he responds. "Uh, because I want to. What's this about?"

Leave it to Quinn to be so vague. He is doing it on purpose. I know that without a doubt. Because of that—and the whole can't get enough rest and I'm stressed—I can't hide my agitation.

"You wanted a baby."

"What the ever-living hell are you talking about?"

"You latched onto me because of the baby. Admit it."

Yes, I know this is insane, but I have apparently lost my mind. I'm sure I can blame it on being pregnant, right?

"I latched onto you because of the baby? That makes no sense."

I know that. But I am not willing to admit it. Not yet.

"That's the only reason you're here in town making nice with me, playing house."

"You think that I would do this all for a baby? I would be able to see my baby no matter what."

"You said it yourself. You wanted kids and your ex didn't."

"And?"

"And now you can have the baby."

He shakes his head and reaches for me, but I dance away.

He drops his hands. "Everly."

I shake my head. "At some point this will all fall apart and pretending now is just stupid."

In the logical part of my brain, I know that this is irrational, that Quinn is a good man, and he would never use me to get a baby. Hell, we didn't even plan on it, and practiced safe sex, so that wasn't his plan. My brain is screaming at me to shut up, but my emotions are a mess, and I can't keep fear from pushing me to do something stupid.

"Just, go away. Just leave me alone."

He studies me for a moment. I know he wants to say something, but he holds it back. Instead, he steps closer, grabbing me and kissing me. I expect it to be brutal, a show of dominance, but again, Quinn knows me too well.

The kiss he gives me a sweet, just a soft brush of his mouth against mine. It only takes seconds, but I melt, right there. My heart turns over and I feel tears filling my eyes.

We stare at each other for just a few seconds. I know I'm wrong, that I'm doing it because I'm afraid, but I can't force myself to apologize. To tell him that I know he isn't there because of the baby. Probably because there is a small part of me that can't understand why he would want to be with me for me.

When I don't say anything, his shoulders sink. He shakes his head, but his gaze never leaves mine when he says, "This isn't over."

He leaves me there, silence filling the air as I sink down on the floor and cry. I know this is all my fault, but I can't bring myself to fix it by chasing him.

24

QUINN

I drive around for over an hour trying to keep my temper under control. I don't know where she comes up with some of the things she thinks about me, other than she is expecting me to be an asshole like Trent. I don't even know the guy's last name and I want to go find him and beat the shit out of him. It was a decade ago, but she can't let go of it.

I find myself turning toward Wyatt's bar. It isn't that busy, but it's late on a Sunday and no matter how different this town is, it's still a small Texas town.

I sigh as I look at the neon sign, trying to decide if I am going to go in or not.

Grady: *Where the fuck are you?*

Oh, I forgot I messaged my brothers when I stormed out of the house.

Me: *Wyatt's.*

Grady: *Be there in a sec.*

Fuck. Does he mean they drove here? About five minutes later, they pull up in Carter's SUV. I roll my eyes, but I would be lying if I said I wasn't happy to have them here. I slip out of my car.

"What the hell are you doing here?"

"You send me a text about handling Syd's moods—which she read because it was sitting on the table in front of her, so you're in so much trouble—and there was no way she was going to let me not come find you. Especially when you don't answer me."

"Sorry. I was driving around trying to cool my temper."

"Uh, yeah, we all know. It's on the Juniper Springs Express," Carter says, holding up his phone.

"How the hell did you get on there?" The app is for residents only. Hell, I haven't gained access to it and I now live here. At least I think I still live here.

"Becca. And in case you wanted to know, she's with Everly."

I sigh, feeling a little better now. I hated being away from her, but after the things she said to me, I needed to step back for an hour or two. I didn't want her to be alone.

"Do you think we'll get a discount?" Carter asks as he walks to the door. "You know, since they're family?"

"Wyatt isn't family. Everly and I will probably not ever get married."

"Mom would smack you upside the head for that comment. You know pieces of paper distributed by the state of Texas don't make you family. You're having a baby together. This is just a bump in the road." This comes from Grady, who never had a long-term relationship before Syd.

"You didn't handle that very well, if memory serves."

WILD LOVE

When Syd got mad and walked out, he had crawled inside of a whiskey bottle.

"Yeah, well, I learned. You will too. Let's go in and talk to the man you came to see."

"And who would that be?" I ask.

"Wyatt. He raised her and he probably knows her best," Gavin says.

That's exactly why I showed up here. What Gavin says is true. Other than Becca, Wyatt probably knows her better than anyone else in her life.

We file in and I take in the scene. It's dark—I mean, a bar is never made to be bright—but there is a classic feel to the place. Dark wood, cushioned booths. The bar looks old, as if it has been there as long as the building. College team flags decorate the walls, along with all the professional teams. My brothers are already heading over to the bar.

I see Wyatt standing there, his arms crossed over this massive chest, giving me a death glare.

"What?"

Yep, I'm being mature. One eyebrow rises as he continues to stare at me. There's some twangy country song blaring on the jukebox and it smells of beer and fried food. Not in a bad way. It was just annoying because I would rather be home with Everly.

"What are you doing here?" he asks, accusation dripping from every syllable he utters.

I open my mouth to tell him exactly what happened, but Gavin steps up.

"Hey there. I don't know if you remember me."

"Yeah."

That's it. I don't know if anyone has ever stopped Gavin flat. He's a slick lawyer with a charming personality—until he has to get mean in court.

"Have you heard from Everly?"

He shakes his head. "It was on JSE."

The short time I have lived in Juniper, I have learned that is the worst app ever invented. "I'm inventing a Jon Howard character for *Sharp Edges* and killing him slowly."

Wyatt's lips twitch. "Half the town would celebrate your book just for that—especially the teenagers."

My brothers are all sitting at the bar, so I do the same. They order beers, I order water. One eyebrow rises again, and I shake my head.

"I'm not adding alcohol to the situation. I'll go back there tonight, and it would be best to be sober."

Wyatt nods and gives me a water. He studies me for a long moment before he asks me the question, "So, tell me what you did to Everly?"

"I didn't do anything to her."

He opens his mouth to argue with me, but Gavin steps in again.

"Listen, maybe take a step back and not argue with him. He came here for advice because you know her."

There is a beat of silence, then he nods. "Go ahead."

"I took her to dinner."

"Which went great," Carter says. "Mom and Dad love her. Like, they might throw one of us overboard to keep her."

"And?" Wyatt asks.

"She started a fight."

"Listen, I know she's ornery."

I snort. "Yeah, that's the understatement of the century. You know what she accused me of?" He opens his mouth, but I keep going and ignore them all. "She claimed I only want her because of the baby. Can you believe that?"

"Well—"

"I mean, it's been less than a week, and I beg your pardon, but I couldn't keep my hands off her from the moment I met her. There's just something there, this spark inside of her, and I'm like some goddamn moth dancing closer and closer until she burns me. And I like it. That's what's so weird. I like that I have to work at it, peel away all the layers and see this amazing woman she is beneath it all."

There is stunned silence for a second.

"Well, that was a lot of words for you," Carter says in a tone that makes it sound like he's praising a five-year-old.

"Yeah, I would have to agree," a voice says from behind me. I glance over and find Mason standing there. Great, exactly what I need. Both her brothers will probably beat the shit out of me. Or at least try.

"Did you tell her all that?" Wyatt asks.

I look at him as Mason takes the barstool next to mine. "Tell her that I'm a moth. I don't think so."

God, I hope I didn't.

"What did you tell her?" Wyatt asks.

"I didn't say anything after she accused me of only wanting her because of the baby. Other than it wasn't over. I just had to get out of there and cool off."

"That's just insane," Carter says. "You guys weren't

around, but before Quinn met Everly, he was a big old bear, not working, not doing anything but being grumpy. Hell, he tagged along with us to Denver because he was avoiding work. But the moment he met her, everything seemed to fall into place. That didn't happen with Elsa."

"Abby," I correct him.

"Whatever."

"Who are Elsa and Abby?" Wyatt asks.

"They are one person. One ice cold witch, otherwise known as his ex-wife."

I don't refute Carter because he's right. I would never call her names, especially now that I see the way I am with Everly. There was something missing out of my marriage and it was warmth. Abby seemed warm—her social media made people think that. I bought into it because I wanted that, needed it. I didn't look enough beneath the surface to realize who she really was.

"Everly is perfect for him," Carter remarks.

"I know that," I say. "I tried to tell her that."

"But did you tell her that you love her?" Grady asks. "They like the declarations."

"I will interject that someone doesn't need to be a woman to want to be told that they are loved," Gavin says.

"Yeah. She didn't declare she loved me."

"Yeah, she did." This comes from Wyatt.

I frown at Wyatt. "What?"

"I pretended that I didn't know that much about her sex life because she is my little sister, and I did help raise her. But I know that she doesn't ever have a two-night stand. I know that she doesn't meet up with men more than once...let alone twice. And she would never let a man move in with her like she did with you, unless she wanted you there. She might have not said the words, but she has put herself out there more than with any other man."

I continue to frown as I think about it. She has let me know how odd it was that she let me hang out. That she kept coming back to me. I let my mind wander back to the conversation we had a few nights ago when she told me about Trent the Asshole and how she had felt so exposed.

She was telling me that I was the first. That no other man in recent years had made her want to take a chance. But she didn't say the words either. So, we're both cowards. I snort.

"Just let him go," I hear Carter explain. "He's one of those deep-water kinds of guys. Has to think everything through. I mean, he's an artist, but he can be anal."

"Shut up," I murmur as I realize just what I am going to have to do. "Thanks."

I get up from the barstool, but Wyatt stops me by calling out to me.

"Where are you going?"

"I'm going to have a little chat with Everly."

"Yes, he is!" Carter yells, but I ignore him and the rest of my brothers. Everly is all I care about and I'm going to make sure she understands that.

25

EVERLY

The first half hour after Quinn left, I lay in bed feeling sorry for myself. I mean, I have a right, right? I was in the right. Right?

Yeah, I know I'm lying to myself, but admitting what a mess I've made of things just isn't something I'm ready for. I do the one thing that I think will make me feel better.

I put a pillow over my face and scream.

"Don't smother yourself!" Becca yells rushing into my bedroom.

"Damn, Becca. You scared me."

She sits down on my bed. "Have you heard from him?"

"Nope. He's probably done with me."

She snorts.

"What?"

The look of disgust she sends my way should shame me, but at the moment, I'm mired in self-pity. "That man is not done with you by a long shot."

"Of course, the baby will keep us tethered forever."

Snorting again, she shakes her head. "That man is over the moon. He's not going anywhere, and it has nothing to do with the baby. It's just an added benefit."

"Yeah, well, I'm not so sure about that."

"I am. Before he knew you were pregnant, he was all over you. Plus, and I mean this with all the love I have in my heart for you, you are not an easy person to love. You push people away more than you bring them in."

I open my mouth to argue with her, but she shakes her head.

"You do and you have your reasons. I'm not saying it's a bad thing. It's just you. But he didn't let that deter him. He got to know you. He enticed you out of your comfort zone. That's why you lashed out at him today."

She stands and walks out of the room. I blink.

"Is that it?"

"Come on, I want to do some snooping."

I follow the sound of her voice and find her going through the supplies and pictures he'd been sketching. He has been working in what I call my home office, which is a bedroom with a desk, my laptop and a couch.

"Becca."

"Oh. Em. GEEEEEE!" She giggles and starts jumping up and down.

"What?"

"It's you."

I sink down on the couch. "Yeah, he draws a lot. It's almost like Mason with cooking. You know Mason is always fiddling in the kitchen? Well, Quinn is like that with drawing. He's always doodling."

It's something that I love about him. Warmth slips through me as I remember watching him sit in my living room and drawing. It gives me a sense of peace just watching him.

"You didn't tell me he put you in *Sharp Edges*."

I blink at her, pulling myself out of my thoughts. "What?"

"It's you with Danvers."

She turns the sketch pad over and shows me. She's right. It's Danvers, who looks a lot like Quinn, then there's me. And under the drawing is the name *Everly Spencer, partner and lover.*

I take the pad from her and she's going through other things.

"Becca, really?"

"Yeah. I want to prove something to you." She keeps going through the other doodles and drawings. "He did."

"He did what?"

She hands me another pad and it's another drawing of me.

"And this proves what?"

"He did these before he knew you were pregnant. See how only your first name is there. It's dated a month ago. He didn't know your last name at that point, so he just used your first name. It was like he was declaring it to the world."

Sure enough, I see the date and do the calculations. It was a trip to Fort Worth. My eyes start to sting.

"What do you mean, declaring it to the world?"

"Everly is not a common name. He wanted everyone to know it was you."

Then, I can't hold back the tears. They are streaming down my face, as I let out a sob.

"Oh, Everly," she says, wrapping her arms around me. "Why would you even think the baby was the only reason he wanted you?"

I shrug, embarrassed even with Becca. I can't tell her how I feel. But she pulls back.

"Tell me."

"I can't think of one reason for him to want to stick around."

"How about the fact that every bit of my soul needs you to be able to breathe?" Quinn says quietly.

I look over my shoulder and he's standing there, leaning against the door jamb, his arms crossed as he watches me. I turn back to Becca, who smiles at me, then nods as she leaves the room. I turn all the way around to watch her go. She stops, rising up to her tiptoes. Quinn leans down and listens as she whispers in his ear. His lips twist up into a smile and he nods. Then, Becca slips out of the room.

For a long moment, we stand there staring at each other. I hear Becca's car start up and still he says nothing.

"What was that?" I ask.

"She threatened me again."

I snort. "She doesn't mean it."

"Yeah, she does, but that's okay by me."

Another long beat of silence fills the air around us. I hold up the drawing pad. "Sorry I went through your things."

His mouth kicks up on one side. "No, you aren't."

I snort again. The man knows me so well. "No, I'm not."

"I don't care. I have nothing to hide from you, Everly." His voice is low and sexy, and it shoots right to my core. I squeeze my thighs together.

"When did you come up with this character?"

He sighs and shifts his weight from foot to foot. For some reason he looks...unsettled. Like he'd rather avoid my question.

"Quinn."

"I'll answer it if you answer just one question."

She crossed her arms beneath her breasts and nods. Once.

"Why did you avoid my texts? Before I came up here the other day."

"I..." a sigh. "I-I was trying to break it off with you."

"So, if I hadn't found you again, thanks to Carter being a pest, I would have never heard from you again?"

I open my mouth to say yes, but I know that would be a lie. And there is one thing I won't do is lie about this. Not to Quinn.

"No. You would have heard from me."

"About the baby?"

"Even if I hadn't been pregnant. But...you scared me, and I was freaking out how attached I was getting."

He nods. "I came up with the character the week after Denver. I know that I should have told you and, granted, people are going to probably start recognizing you as soon as it comes out."

"And who is she? Did you just draw me into the book?"

He shakes his head. "You're the new partner."

I blink and stare at him. "So, before California and Ft Worth and the baby, you had already added me to your book?"

"Yeah, I'm really sorry I didn't clear it with you and if you insist, I'll take the character out. I mean, I would have to push back the due date—again."

"What do you mean again?"

"I was…well, it's embarrassing because I had blown past two deadlines."

"For your work? You're never late."

"How do you know that?"

"You're only one of my favorite authors. Being in the business, you hear things." I pause and when he doesn't answer, I prod him more. "Tell me."

"I was lost. Like I couldn't write or draw. Then I met you and everything seemed to work."

I sigh. That's why he was drawing me.

"No, don't do that," he says, walking forward and taking the pad from me and setting it on the desk. He takes my hand, tugging me behind him until we're in my bedroom.

"Sit down, I have a story to tell you."

"Quinn…"

The look he gives me has me blinking. I do as he orders.

"My marriage was kind of crap."

"Yeah, I got that."

"We weren't meant to be married, and I didn't see how bad it was until I walked out on her."

"You walked out?"

He nods "She was so toxic. I had blown past my first deadline and she didn't care. Couldn't give a crap. She was annoyed because I canceled a trip to Aruba. I couldn't go on vacation when I hadn't been doing any work."

I remember what he said earlier and nod. It fits with the image of the ex. "Well, yeah. Your fans would be out for blood. Remember what happened to Martin?"

"Exactly. They are brutal, but it isn't just that. I owed my publisher, my agent, my editor, everyone I worked with to be professional. She didn't see it that way. All she cared about was the notoriety. People might not know who I am from my face, but they know the name. And in New York, the Hawthorne name goes a long way if they realize I am one of *those* Hawthornes."

I nod. "But you would never rest on your laurels."

"Exactly. When I tried to explain it to her, she got pissy, and insisted that we go anyway. She threatened a divorce over it."

"What an idiot."

He smiles. "Yeah, well it wasn't the first time she tried that kind of emotional blackmail. She knew that I had a hang-up about divorce. My parents have been married forever. You saw them."

I smile at the disgust in his voice. The two of them are always touching.

"Yeah. It's sweet."

"Ugh. Anyway, she knew that I didn't want to get divorced, but that wasn't true. I was in our marriage as long as both of us were working at it. I realized she didn't care as long as the money kept flowing. That, along with waiting to have kids—which I now wonder if she ever wanted to have—was too much. So, I walked out."

"Wow."

"And I know that you think I'm with you because of the baby, but I'm not. I mean, I'm here for the baby no matter what, but, Jesus, Everly, you are not an easy woman to deal with. Do you think that I would be here if I didn't love you for you?"

And just like that, I feel tears burning the backs of my eyes again.

"Quinn." That's it. I've never had a man say that to me, other than the idiots I'm related to and the Golds. Definitely not in the romantic way.

"And I know that you're going to argue with me, but you can go ahead and argue all you want. I'm not leaving. *Ever*. You'll be sick of me by the time you accept that you are mine for the rest of our lives."

I open my mouth to tell him how I feel but he's not having it. Not at the moment. He takes my hands and tugs me up off the mattress.

"I love your insane rules, and mood swings. I love that you know exactly what cuss word works for every situation, and I love your t-shirts with sarcastic sayings. But there are other parts of you that I love as well. You might have this hard outer shell, but you are soft and gooey in the middle."

Irritation surges. "What the hell?"

"And I love that I knew you would say that. But you *are* sweet, for those you love. Which makes me think you at least like me a little bit."

I sigh, my heart singing, but I'm not ready to give in, just yet. He picks up on it.

"Okay, here we go. I will not ask you to marry me," he says.

"You don't want to marry me?"

From the lopsided smile, the one I love the most, he knows I'm just busting his balls.

"Oh, I do. You're the one with the hang up about it. Not me. The ball is in your court. When you're ready to marry, I'm ready and willing. If you never want to, it doesn't matter. I will be here forever and ever, until the day I die. I don't care if we end up having ten kids."

"Let's not lose our minds here," I say laughing, my vagina spasming at the thought.

"I will live in sin for the rest of our lives if you want to. If you change your mind, I will be happy to marry you."

This man. He knows exactly what to say to me, how to handle me. And there is a part of me that will always worry about that. I know that without announcing it and apparently, he does too.

"Come here," I say, curling my finger.

"Is that a yes you will let me stay? Or am I going to have to bunk with one of your brothers?"

"Like they would let you," I say with a laugh.

"Wyatt's the one who helped me. I mean, my brothers were there, but Wyatt helped."

I'm not sure how I feel about that, but for now, Quinn is here. That's all that matters. Since he hasn't gotten any closer to me, I sigh, grab his hand, and tug him onto the mattress.

"So," I say leaning over him, "you love me, huh?"

He's smiling and nodding, and even though I hate to say it, I let it go.

"From the moment I met you, you were different. You crawled into my heart, and I didn't realize it at the time, but it's like I've been waiting for you my entire life. I love you, Quinn Matthew Hawthorne."

Then I dip my head to kiss him, to show him just how much I love him.

26

QUINN

A month later, I'm officially moved into Everly's house. I asked if she wanted to keep my San Antonio house and she didn't, so I put it on the market. I was staying up here full-time anyway, but I had an offer the first week it went on sale. So, I sold off most of my furniture, except the massive king size bed. Everly had wanted to keep that.

And now after another month, we're hosting our first dinner. I did most of the cooking, as Everly hates to cook, and she was really honest about it. She sucks at it. I mean, she paid no attention to the water boiling for pasta one night and let it boil away and almost ruin the pan. Part of that might be the fact that she has pregnancy brain.

"I like this backyard," Carter says, taking a swig of beer.

I glance over at him. "No."

"What?"

"You are not moving into the guest room permanently."

"I have a house, thank you very much."

That much is true, but there is definitely something going on with him. "What's up?"

He jerks a shoulder.

"Carter."

"It's not the same in San Antonio without you. And Grady is putting all kinds of rules on me."

I try not to laugh at him. I know he portrays himself as a devil may care kind of guy, but I know that's not all he is. He's deeply committed to our family and his brothers. With all of us paired off he must feel a little lost.

I hear a woman laugh and watch Carter's head whip around. I follow his line of sight and see Piper talking with Everly. He mutters something to himself.

"What was that?"

"What was what?" Grady says, stepping up.

"Nothing," Carter mumbles, decidedly turning his back on the women. It's odd behavior, but that has been happening more and more lately. We still don't know the story of what happened between him and Piper all those years ago.

"Is this a Hawthorne brother meeting," Gavin says stepping up, Oliver next to him.

"Carter was complaining I'm living here." I look at Carter again. "Why don't you buy a house up here?"

He frowns. "There's probably not much to pick from."

"Well, we have an in with the two top house flippers on TV," Grady says, motioning to where Travis Fillmore and Nancy Howard are standing. "They probably know about anything that might be available. Talk to Dad too.

He and Mom were talking about having a house up here, just something small."

"They are?"

Grady nods. "We'll probably end up here at some point. And then there's the grandkid they will want to spoil. Mom's made noises about competing with—and I quote—Everly's hot surrogate mother."

Becca's mom is kind of hot for a mom, so I can see that. She has that bohemian vibe.

"Mom shouldn't feel as if she is competing. They are both MILFs," Carter says.

"Carter!" All three of us yell.

"What? I know that all of you have hang ups, but our mom is hot. There is nothing wrong with admitting it."

"Who are we talking about?" Everly asks, slipping in beside me. She's starting to show, and it's the cutest thing. She hates when I get all mushy about it, but I can't help it.

"I was telling them that our mom is a MILF."

"Inappropriate, but true."

"See!" Carter says, taking Everly by the hand and pulling her in for a hug. "Run away with me. He doesn't deserve you."

She chuckles. "True, but then no man is good enough for me."

Carter leans back. "You are the most amazing woman. I hope you have a girl. It's going to be so much fun having a little Everly stomping around and repeating your comments. Which, of course, are all true."

"Why don't you let go of my woman, and go inside to get the potato salad?"

"It would help," Everly says. She might not think she

has a mother's instincts, but she shows it every time we are together with Carter. Carter can't help but want to help. It's in his nature.

"Let's go pal. I know that there's some sweets we need to bring out too," Grady says, slapping Carter on the back.

They start bickering as they walk away with Oliver and Gavin.

"It all smells good," Everly says looking down at the grill.

I dip my head so that only she can hear me. "Not as good as you smell."

I smile when her face flushes. It's hard to get her to blush, but lately, whenever I reference something I said during sex, she seems to get flustered.

"Behave," she murmurs.

"That's the first time you've asked me to do that."

"Do what?" Mason asks. He's here before he goes back in for the dinner rush, along with Wyatt, who is tossing Carter nasty looks as he brings out food.

"Behave."

Mason looks at her. "You're trying to get him to behave? Those pregnancy hormones are really making you loopy."

She doesn't say anything for a second, then she sniffs. She covers her face with her hands. As expected, Mason freaks out. I have found that neither of her brothers can handle the tears, but Mason isn't good with discerning when they are real and when they are not.

"Aw, shit, I'm sorry, Everly."

"Just go away. Go bother someone else."

He frowns, but he heads on over to talk to Becca and Piper.

"Evie, that was mean," Wyatt says, humor lacing his voice.

Everly chuckles and drops her hands. "Yeah, well, he needs to quit being a dick."

"Agreed. Do you need any help?" He directs the question to me. Since the night I showed up at his bar, we've become friendlier. A week ago, he thanked me for not being an asshole like Carter. That's progress in my opinion.

"Naw, I put my brothers to work," I say motioning to them bringing out the food. "Besides, Becca said something about wanting to talk to you."

"Becca?"

I nod.

He takes off in her direction. For today's cookout, she's dressed like a farmer. Well, a farmer if maybe that farmer was also a gamer who loved everything about 80's culture. Her hair is up in pigtails. The neon pink overalls —which are shorts—and the lime green t-shirt should clash, but they somehow go great together. She's completed the look with Chucks that match perfectly.

"And people think I'm the mean one," Everly says.

I chuckle. "Maybe we're just a matching set."

Her eyes dance with happiness. "I think you might be right." She wraps her arms around me, and I feel something move in her stomach.

"What the hell was that?"

She chuckles and looks up at me, now with real tears

in her eyes. "That, Mr. Hawthorne, is your demon spawn."

I feel my eyes widen. "Really?"

She nods as she takes my hand and places it on her stomach. "Right there, Daddy."

I feel the soft movement.

"He's hungry."

I shake my head. "She's hungry."

Yeah, I want a girl, and she, of course, wants a boy.

I pull her in and wrap my arms around her. "I love you, Everly Spencer."

"I love you, Seven."

I chuckle as I press my mouth to hers.

"Get a room!"

That of course comes from Carter. We're laughing when we break apart. Our friends are all smiling at us, our surrogate family in a way. I look down at Everly and she smiles up at me.

Life will never be better than this.

EPILOGUE 1

EVERLY

Two months later

"You didn't have to come with me," I say, as I settle back on the exam table.

Carter shakes his head. "Quinn is busy on that call."

"And I'm an adult who can go to appointments by myself."

"No."

I blink. He's been...weird since the night of our dinner party. I don't know much, but Quinn said Piper and Carter were childhood friends. He had avoided Piper like she had a plague that would make his dick fall off. And he didn't flirt that much, which was really weird.

There's a sharp knock at the door before it opens revealing Piper.

She's a pretty woman with a wealth of red hair, most of which is up in a bun on top of her head. She's wearing her reading glasses, so there is a whole librarian vibe about her.

"Everly," she says, her bright blue gaze moving on to Carter. "And Carter."

She said Quinn's brother's name with a lot less enthusiasm.

"How are you feeling?" she asks as she walks over to the antibacterial lotion dispenser.

"Doing okay," Carter says.

She rolls her eyes as she rubs her hands together spreading the lotion. "I was talking to Everly."

"I'm doing fine."

"I saw your iron is doing well, so the supplements seem to be working."

"Yeah."

"Any other symptoms? How's the nausea?"

"Not so bad. I've learned to have crackers on the nightstand waiting for me in the morning. But it seems to be not as intense. Smells are still bothering me."

"That's good, and that heightened sense of smell will stick with you for a while."

"Isn't nausea normal?"

That comes from Carter, who is standing beside me frowning.

"Mostly. Some women have none at all."

"That's bullshit," I say. She laughs.

"And then there are the poor women who have it all the way through their pregnancy."

I shudder. "God, that sounds like a nightmare."

"It can be. When the mother is sick like that, we have to make sure the baby is getting the nutrients he needs." She pulls out her tape measure and I lift up my shirt.

"You seem to be doing well from the results of all the blood work."

"Good. I've changed a few things in my diet as you suggested."

"Excellent. Let's check out that baby."

It doesn't take her long to get through the exam. From what she says, the baby is right on schedule, if a little big even with the adjusted due date. Then she grabs the heartbeat doppler thing.

"So, Uncle Carter, want to hear the baby's heartbeat?"

He looks at me, then back at her. "Really? It won't hurt her?"

Her expression softens just a bit. "I would never do that, but that's very sweet."

"Then, hot damn, yes."

That's the most Carter has said since Piper entered the room. She grabs the jelly and squirts it on my stomach. It takes a little bit of work, but she finds the little shit…I mean, my baby.

"Ah, there you are, baby Spencer-Hawthorne."

She's been calling it that every appointment.

"That sounds like a horse galloping," Carter says, his voice filled with wonder.

She laughs. "Yeah, that's exactly how I describe it." She wipes off my stomach. "I want you to set up another sonogram in a couple months, but right now, I think we can just get you back in here in a month. I want a call at any worries. We have a nursing staff that can talk you through anything, and they'll make sure to bring me on board if needed."

She washes her hands. "Do you have any questions?"

"Yes," Carter says. "How many people can be in the delivery room? Quinn says I can't be there."

"Carter," I say, not even trying to hide my exasperations. "We both said you couldn't be in there."

He crosses his arms over his chest. "Gavin refuses to have his baby and this might be my only chance."

"Mainly because he's a man, and he's married to a man."

"And I wanted to see it."

"Well, I don't want you to."

Piper saves me from smacking Quinn's brother around.

"Carter," she waits until he finally looks at her. "That day is going to be stressful. Seriously, it's a wonderful event, but for Everly, it will be a lot of hard work. Your... enthusiasm might be too much, especially for Everly, who is very private."

I had a feeling she was measuring every word she said.

He sighs. "Great, now whenever Syd has babies, I have to convince her. She's a harder sell than Everly."

He might be right there. I might be a badass, but Syd has an extra helping of it, and she's been dealing with Carter longer than I have.

After setting up my next appointment, I take Carter to get a milkshake. Yes, I know. I treat him like a kid, but he is like a kid. I took the day off because it is Monday and we just hired new help at the store. We had the money and we realized that I would have to take some time off.

"Well?" Quinn asks as he scoops me up into one of his

amazing hugs. I'm still not used to them, but I am getting that way.

"Piper refuses to let me in the delivery room."

He chuckles, releasing me from the hug but keeps his arm around me. "I should have known that was why you wanted to be at the appointment. You should know better than to ask Piper."

"That and I got to hear the baby's heartbeat."

"Pretty cool, huh?"

He nods. "I have to go make some calls."

He walks out the back door.

"It's hard to believe he's responsible for millions of dollars," I say.

Quinn smiles. "I think he makes that kind of money because he is the way he is. He thinks outside of the box. It was his idea to start branching out."

"Really?"

He nods.

"How did your meeting go?"

Quinn is in talks with a few companies who are interested in making Sharp Edges a series.

"Really well, although I'm not sold yet."

I cock my head to the side. "Not sold on it?"

"The person they want to run the show has issues in his background."

"Issues?"

"Let's just say, Me Too would have a field day with him."

I nod. "It'll happen."

"Meanwhile, I did clear it with my publisher to have a big release party at Nerdvana."

I blink. "What do you mean by that?'

"They are pushing up the release date since so many people really want to see what's up with this new character—thanks to Becca."

Becca convinced him to hire a social media expert to handle Quinn's social media platforms, mainly his Insta. He's gained thousands of followers in just a few short weeks. But we were happy that the release was going to be after the demon spawn was born. That way I could travel with him.

"Pushing it up? How far up and how irritated am I going to be?"

He wraps his arms around me, pulling me flush to his body. "You are always irritated—which turns me on, of course. But it would be right before the baby was born. It's the only signing I have agreed to do."

I blink. "Quinn, you need to go out."

He shakes his head. "No. I don't need them and if preorders are anything to go by, they are okay with it. Plus, it gives us a chance to push it at Comic-Con."

"The Comic-Con. San Diego?"

I've never been able to go. We've gone to quite a few around here, but we had never been able to score tickets to the big dance.

"Yep. Better yet, I made sure that Nerdvana will be represented."

"What's that mean?"

"Becca is going to talk on a couple of panels."

My eyes widen.

"And I got you a little bit of promo with the publisher. They're going to talk to you all next week about it."

"Quinn, I didn't ask for that."

"No, you didn't. That's what makes this so delicious. And stop that. I can see that you're trying to come up with a way to make this bad. My editor is over the moon about supporting a female-run business. Good image for the company."

"When you say close to the baby's birthday, how close?"

"Four weeks. We can release the book, have all the fun stuff with that, then we will have the baby."

QUINN

3 weeks & 4 days before due date

THIS RELEASE PARTY IS INSANE.

I should have known it would be. Thanks to my social media expert Avery O'Bryan, the buildup to the release had everyone ready to lose their minds. My readers turned out in force, and Juniper Springs welcomed them with open arms.

The sheriff's department worked with us to make sure everything was done safely, and they have a couple of their deputies here tonight. We worked with lodging and food services to offer specials to keep people here in town, instead of going back to San Antonio or Austin. According to Becca, I'm everyone's favorite new resident thanks to that.

My entire family is here for it and Everly's would be too, but their businesses are too busy for them to be here.

"Have I ever told you how proud I am?" Everly asks. I glance over at her. Warmth steals through me at the sight of her. She insisted on being here, even though Piper had ordered her on bed rest. In fact, the look she got from Piper told me the doctor wasn't happy. But she's been off her feet the entire time. She's decked out in her favorite shirt of the moment that reads Evil spawn percolating. Do not disturb.

"You have," I say, leaning forward and brushing my mouth over hers. I have my hand on her stomach and feel our daughter kick my hand.

She sighs. "I kind of love that she does that, but it also creeps me out."

"Creeps you out?"

"I mean, she's responding to her father kissing me. Isn't that...I don't know...gross?"

"She's responding to the love you feel for me, not the sexual feelings."

"I guess so." Her hand goes to her back, which isn't that uncommon these days, but she's been doing it more today than I've seen.

"Are you okay?"

She nods. "Just a little tired. I was thinking that maybe Carter could take me home."

"I can do that, then I can stay there."

She giggles. "Your family has reservations at Mason's."

Which isn't normally allowed, but Mason allowed it because we're family.

I like the sound of that. The brothers have gotten pulled into our family texts now, and I heard Mom complaining about needing more women in the group to fight off the influx of testosterone.

Then, an expression I have never seen comes over Everly's face. Fear and pain seem to fill her eyes. Alarm races through me.

"What?"

She shakes her head and starts deep breathing.

"Piper!"

The doctor hurries over. "What is it?"

"I don't know, but her face doesn't look like it's anything good."

"Really, Quinn? That's how you describe it?" Everly asks with just enough irritation that my nerves settle a little.

"How far apart?" Piper demands.

"Just this first one," Everly says, taking my hand and sitting down. "But, in the words of my bestie, it sucked all the balls."

"Any other symptoms?"

"No. Well, my lower back has been bothering me, but you know that's been a problem these last few weeks."

Piper nods. Everyone is crowding around us now that they have figured out something is going on.

"Why don't we go back to the office?" I suggest.

"Good thinking," Piper says. "Can someone get my bag? It's in my car."

Becca pops up. "I'll do it." She takes Piper's keys and hurries away.

Once we have her settled on the couch and I close the door to keep our friends and family out.

"So, what we need to do is time contractions. There's no reason to rush to the hospital."

Panic hits me hard, my heart galloping and sweat popping out on my forehead. "No reason? What the actual f—"

"Quinn, unless the water breaks, I can stay comfortably at home for the first few hours."

"Hours?"

I feel faint.

"Don't pass out on me, big guy," Piper says. The door then smashes open, and I turn with a snarl at whoever dared open the door.

Becca's eyes widen. "Oh, boy, you look scary, Quinn. Here, Piper."

She hands the bag over to Piper, but before she can rifle through it, Everly groans. "Here comes another one."

Piper frowns and times the contraction.

"Okay, that was really fast for just the second one, less than five minutes. I would feel better if we were at the hospital."

"You just said we could wait. What is it!" I yell the last three words and the entire office goes silent.

"Ladies, go on out and get the troops ready to move. I have a feeling they will want to tag along," Everly says, her calm voice sending a wave of embarrassment through me.

I sigh, telling myself to calm down. I look at Piper. "I'm sorry."

"Hey, Quinn, this isn't anything new. Dads freak out all the time. Everything is going to be okay."

Once we are alone, Everly reaches out and I help her

off the couch. She wraps her arms around me. "Everything is going to be okay, Seven."

Her calm voice, the way she's rubbing my back, has my entire body relaxing.

"If you say so."

She chuckles and looks up at me, tears in her eyes. "You were calm as could be when I told you I was pregnant, but you freak out now."

I kiss her forehead. "Let's get to the hospital."

She nods and brushes her mouth against mine. "I love you."

Three hours later I'm holding Esme Victoria Spencer-Hawthorne. She has her mommy's dark hair and definitely her lungs. She was loud right after birth as if letting us know she was going to be as ornery as her mother.

"She's tiny," Carter says. I nod.

"She didn't feel tiny coming out," Everly says, her dark amusement making me chuckle. I look at the love of my life, happiness filling me. She made it through labor like a champ, giving birth less than an hour after we got to the hospital. I should have known that Esme wasn't going to wait around for anyone else's timeline.

"All this hair," Carter muses, his fingers dancing over the soft fuzz.

"It's my turn," my mom says.

"Again?"

"Shut up and give me the baby and no one will get hurt."

Everly laughs, then moans. "Don't make me laugh. It still hurts."

"Does anyone want anything? I need something to munch on," Carter says. No one wants anything so he heads out in search of snacks.

"What is up with that boy?" my mom asks. No one has an answer —other than Grady's 'he's fucked in the head as usual.'

It takes us another hour to get rid of everyone. It's finally quiet and Everly and Esme are both sleeping. I had my mom go pick up my drawing pad at the store, and I sit in the chair sketching both my girls as they doze.

"I'm not sure you have permission to do that," Everly murmurs.

"I can convince you it's worth it."

Her eyes open slowly and just like the first time I watched her wake, I fall in love with her all over again. I should have known that I was a goner the moment I met her.

"What is going on in that creative mind of yours?" she asks.

"I was thinking of our weekend in Denver. About how I should have known you were the woman for me."

"And how would you have known that?"

"You were wild and free, and for the first time in my life, I wanted that too. But I wanted it with you."

Her eyes fill with tears.

"It's true. And now, you have given me another wild girl to love."

I take her hand as I sit down on the bed. I bring it up to my mouth, brushing my mouth over her knuckles.

A man couldn't ask for more than that.

EPILOGUE 2
CARTER

The excitement of the night should have worn me out, but with a new Hawthorne in the family, I can't settle down. Of course, we're all at the hospital still. It worked out that we were all here for Quinn's release party.

I step out of the room in search of something to gnaw on. I know that the cafeteria is closed, so I'm hoping for a snack machine or something. I also need some caffeine.

"What are you doing skulking around the hallways, Carter?" Piper asks.

I take a moment to compose myself before I turn to face her. If I don't, she might figure out just how I feel about her.

When I'm ready, or I think I am, I turn. Of course, my body immediately responds to her. It's the middle of the night, and she was in there for three hours for Everly's labor and delivery, and she looks amazing. Fair skin, light green eyes, that sprinkling of freckles over her nose...she always gets to me.

"Looking for something to eat."

She smiles and shakes her head. "You always did have a high metabolism."

"Like you don't?" I motion to her body.

"I work out six days a week."

"When do you have time for that?"

She cocks her head to the side studying me as if I'm a specimen. I hope she doesn't look too deeply.

"About five in the morning."

"So," I say holding up some money. "Know where the good snack machine is?"

"Of course, I do," she says with a laugh. She straightens, then motions with her hand. "Come on. It's on the next floor up."

I walk her into the stairwell and follow her up, which is torture. This woman has the most amazing backside known to man and the way her scrubs pull tight with each step, I might just pass out. She opens the door on the next floor and looks back at me, but not fast enough for me to raise my gaze off her ass.

"Really, Carter?"

I feel my face heat, but I shrug. "Sorry, but you do have an amazing ass."

She says nothing else, but I do get an eye roll.

We make it down the hall of what looks to be mostly examination rooms.

"Why are you here?" I ask her.

"I delivered your niece."

It's my turn to roll my eyes. "No, I mean, in Juniper."

"Oh." She steps into an alcove that has snack and soda machines. I start looking over the offerings.

"So, Juniper?"

"I was ready for a change."

"Where were you?"

I know exactly where she was. I happened to see her just once in New York and then I started obsessing over her like a weirdo. I didn't call her like a normal person would have. No, instead I stalked her on social media and dropped a few hints here and there when I was talking to my mother.

"New York. I was there for the worst of the pandemic. After that, I decided I wanted to be near my parents no matter how much they drive me crazy."

"Juniper seems like small potatoes."

"Mrs. Howard offered me good money to relocate. I don't have to pay for my office."

I stop looking over the offerings and turn to her. "Estella Howard?"

She nods. Nancy Howard works for my family, and I've dealt with her grandmother a time or two. I knew there was more to that old bird than she let people know.

"They were just building this hospital with the birthing center. It's small, but I get to know my patients. I like that."

It's hard to be like this, trying to find out what has been going on with her. I mean, I stalk her on social media, but it's the most I do right now. I need to know more, but I don't have that right. Not anymore. I lost it when I walked away from our friendship, but at the age of thirteen, I wasn't ready for her to be in my life as just a friend. I never got a chance to explain why.

I open my mouth to say something—anything—to get her to stay. Piper has other ideas.

"Well, it's been a long day and Wilbur is waiting for me."

"Wilbur?" Who the fuck is Wilbur?

She nods. "Only man I need in my life."

Again, I want to ask more questions, but I don't have a chance.

"Night, Carter."

And then I'm watching her walk away from me, unable to come up with something to get her attention.

Seems like nothing ever changes, but the moment she turns the corner at that end of the hall, I tell myself, I will come up with something to get her attention. What, I have no idea, but I will not lose her again.

THANK YOU FOR READING WILD LOVE! IF YOU LOVED THE book, please think about leaving a review at your favorite online retailer or review site!

Want to see a flash forward of Wild Love? Just join my newsletter to get the flash forward:

New Members—>Give Me My Book

Current Members—> Give Me My Book

Want to know what happens with Carter? His book is coming in soon! Make sure to subscribe to my newsletter or my RSS feed to keep up to date!

This book is in the Camos and Cupcakes world and starts with the book DELICIOUS.

Get the book that readers call a *"...fun, fast pace and steamy romance..."* and *"...laugh out loud funny."*

One click today—>DELICIOUS.

Enjoy the first chapter!

ALLISON

I don't know when I fell in love with Ed Cooper.

Scratch that.

I do know. I was thirteen and my brother brought his friend back from basic training. Ed was tall, sweet, and had red hair. RED HAIR. I've always had a thing for guys with red hair. Okay, it all sort of started with Ed, but I'd always found redheads attractive. While friends were drooling over Harry Potter—who was out as an infatuation because he shares a name with my brother—I was crushing on the Weasley twins. Not Ron because, well, he's Ron and he whines, and I don't like whiners. Also, why would I ever want a boyfriend who thought a rat was a good companion pet? And, said pet wasn't really a rat.

But I digress. Back to my infatuation.

Ed Cooper, delectable ginger.

Now that I'm within spitting distance of my thirties, I realize, it's a little stupid to be this infatuated with a man who treats me like his little sister. Wait, does that say something about me? Ew, don't go there, Allison.

My infatuation has gotten worse with each passing year. It isn't like I haven't had dates or that I'm pining away saving my virginity for him. I've had sex. Lots of it. Okay, not a lot... only with two guys...and it was pretty boring with both of them. I'm not a virgin, which was the point of my comment.

I step into the mansion that has been renovated into a small mall of sorts. It sits in the heart of the King William District in San Antonio that is dominated by gothic architecture. It's become a hip kind of place for specialty shops and restaurants. It's why my brother and his two friends, Fritz O'Bryan and Ed Cooper, decided to open Camos and Cupcakes there. Close enough to the military bases but also in an area that a lot of tourists frequent. I tend to be here several days a week. I step into the bakery and draw in a deep breath, letting the sugary sweetness fill my senses and buoy my spirits. This is the first day of my staycation. I love to travel and the fact that I cannot really do that this year is kind of a bummer. I bought my house last year, and this year I saved up to buy my brand-new Malibu with all the bells and whistles, so I honestly couldn't afford a real vacation. Plus, the only time I could get off for a while is next week. Neither of my friends can go, and I'm just not the sort of woman who would go on vacation by myself. I would get bored, because I like to share experiences. And talk. A lot.

So, I'm here to kick off my staycation with a treat.

There's a crowd but that's normal. This place is always hopping on Saturday mornings. It doesn't take me long to find Ed. He's hard to miss in any crowd. He tops 6'4" but it isn't that. I know that I would be able to find him anywhere. And, all that red hair helps. It's longer now than when he was in the military and is given to curl. I'd love to slip my fingers through the silky strands. I curl my fingers into my hand to control the need. Another aspect of his new life is the full beard. I've never been a woman who likes a man with facial hair, but I love it on Ed. As usual, he's wearing an apron with the title of their bakery splashed across the front of it. Flour and chocolate color the white material. He's been busy, as he is five days a week. See, Ed Cooper just isn't only the man I've been in love with for fifteen years. He's a baker. A cupcake baker. And not just any cupcake baker. He's considered one of the top bakers in San Antonio. Five days a week, he creates sugary, decadent treats.

I call him my own personal Ginger Jesus.

Now, you might be thinking that he's some kind of wimpy kind of guy. Not that I think bakers are wimpy, but Ed is probably the opposite of what most people would think of a baker. He's sexy as sin, tatted up with skulls, still sports a six-pack, and rides a Harley.

I watch him scan the bakery, looking over the customers. There's more than a shop keeper's interest to his gaze, which makes sense. Ed, Fritz, and my brother are all former Army. They inspect areas the same way whether they are in the shop or out on the River Walk. They cannot help it. Some things just become second nature, even after trading their uniforms for aprons.

The moment his gaze settles on me, my body temperature escalates into overheating territory. A slow, sexy smile curves his lips. Oh, goodness. Just like the first time he looked at me, I feel my heart dance a little jig and my face heats up, not to mention my pussy tightening. I walk around with wet panties whenever I'm near Ed. Or thinking about him. So, like, almost all the time.

I remind myself that he isn't for me, never will be. He's...unattainable. He'll always see me as that flat-chested, frizzy-haired teenager who couldn't say hi to him without blushing.

Same story, different decade—although with boobs and better hair.

Anytime I complain about the lack of sex in my life, my best friend EJ claims I will never find another man. Not while I'm infatuated with Ed. Still, I'm here to kick off my staycation and I want a treat. Meaning the cupcake. Not the man who made them. Not really.

Damn.

I push my way through the crowd, and when I arrive at the counter, there it is. A strawberry lemonade cupcake sits next to a cup of coffee. I know he doctored it with the right amount of cream. That's how well he knows me. I look up at him and he gives me an understanding smile.

"Thanks, Ed." I pull out a ten, but he shakes his head.

"I can't charge you for your namesake cupcake."

Yes, he even named a cupcake after me.

Like I said. Ginger. Freaking. Jesus.

"Thank you."

"Your friends are back there," he says pointing over my head.

I glance over my shoulder. EJ and Savannah are sitting at a corner table. They wave me over and I want to go, but I also want to stay near Ed. He smells like sex and vanilla. But definitely not vanilla sex. I'm pretty sure Ed has never had vanilla sex. Of course, I'm thinking about vanilla and sex and that leads to me wondering if he uses frosting during sex. If so, what flavor?

Jesus, what is wrong with me?

"Thanks again, Ed," I say, picking up my cupcake and coffee. I make my way over to my friends.

I set my coffee on the table just as EJ jumps up out of her chair and pulls me into a warm embrace. Taller than me by a good five inches, the bookstore owner gives the best hugs. I held my cupcake away from her so not to ruin it but returned the hug with all my might using my free arm.

She pulls back and smiles at me. EJ always seems larger than life. Not because she is curvy. She has that kind of personality. Funny, warm, EJ is beautiful both in spirit and body. She dresses like a bohemian and talks faster than I thought humanly possible, unless you were a character on the Gilmore Girls. With her deep Georgia accent, it is sometimes difficult to understand her. Today, she's wearing her red hair down, the curls spilling over her shoulders.

"Doing okay?" she asks.

I nod. Savannah smiles up at me. "Sit down before you collapse. I think you need some sugar."

"Gee, you're so warm and inviting."

My other best friend snorts and flips me off. Savannah Martinez, the youngest and most talented of the Martinez Restaurant family. While EJ is open and boisterous, Savannah is pessimistic and quiet. I'm truly touched that she is here after closing the night before. Saturday mornings are for sleeping in Savannah's world.

"Be nice or I won't treat you to your favorite tonight."

My mouth waters. "Cheese enchiladas?"

"Yeah. And I took tonight off, which is a big thing."

And it is. Savannah is the head chef for her family's most successful restaurant. Taking a Saturday night off is not a normal thing, especially the weekend before Cinco de Mayo. Their restaurant will definitely be packed with idiots.

"Thank you."

"I think we should go to La Trinidad," Savannah says. Her family owns the restaurant, and while Savannah oversees all their restaurants, La Trinidad is the one she works in. "We can drink Austin's margaritas, then make him drive us home."

Savannah's oldest brother makes the best margaritas.

"That sounds like a plan."

"What are you three planning?" my brother Harry asks as he leans down and kisses the top of my head. He's four years older, but we're closer than most other siblings I know. It came from what we endured together as children while our mother was sick. That fear never really leaves you after one of your parents fights for their life.

He's wearing trousers and a white shirt, his custom uniform. There's no reason to dress so nice since all he does is handle the books for Camos and Cupcakes, but Harry likes to dress like he has a real job. His words, not mine. I know. He's kind of anal, but I still love him. Most of the time.

"I'm going to eat my cupcake, then we are going to go out tonight for dinner. I take it after EJ gets done with the shop?" I raise one eyebrow in question.

EJ nods. "Yeah. Sammy's closing tonight."

"You're going to leave her on her own?" I ask. Sammy

is a sweet college student, but she has the air of absent-minded professor about her.

"Naw. I hired another pretty boy. He'll keep her company."

"Do you always use derogatory terms for men like that?" My brother asks without malice.

"It's not. He is pretty and he's twenty, so he is a boy. And he's good at work."

"So, you're going out too, Savannah?" he asks.

"Yeah," she says, looking down at her phone with a frown. She's not being rude, she's being Savannah. Her family's business makes it impossible for her to ever get away. There are constant texts and emails and while my job as a chemo nurse can kick my ass, I don't think I would ever be able to deal with Savannah's life.

"I've been promised cheese enchiladas and Austin Margaritas."

They weren't a thing but that's what I call them. I am going to drink my weight in them since I won't have Ed's frosting to eat. And, of course, that leads to other thoughts and euphuisms. I really do need to find a man.

"So, no guys?" he asks.

"No. Absolutely not. We want no men horning in on our fun."

"What about Austin?" he asks.

"He doesn't count," I say.

"I think he might disagree with you," Savannah says, humor lacing her words.

"You know what I mean. He's our margarita man. MM." I like that acronym. I think we need to start calling him that.

"Well, make sure you call me if you three need a ride home," he says. I might be almost thirty, but my brother still sees me as a tween who needs to check in.

"Thank you. Now, go away. I'm sure you have numbers to crunch."

He laughs and leaves us to our cupcakes.

"I have no idea why he puts up with you," Savannah says.

"He has too. We're blood. Plus, I'm still holding the goods on a few stories that can be used as blackmail. I know it. He knows it."

I slip my finger over the icing lightly, just skimming a little of the sugary sweetness off the top. I lick my finger and bite back a hum. Barely. The fresh strawberry frosting is light and sweet and...damn. Just that little taste has my head thinking of all kinds of bad things. I imagine that he made this cupcake in particular for me—wearing nothing but an apron.

"You're both adults. I have a feeling that blackmail time is past," EJ says.

"You have no siblings, so you have no idea. Tell her, Savannah."

Savannah pulls her attention back from ger phone and looks at me, then EJ. "She's probably right. Plus, Harry is so OCD it'll drive him crazy not to tie up all those loose ends."

"What the hell does that mean?" EJ asks. She truly has no idea what we're talking about.

"There's this thing between siblings. It's primal. We all fight for attention from our parents until they die. Knowing my brothers and sister, they would probably even figure out a way to get back at me after my parents leave earth," Savannah says.

"And, let's be honest. Part of the fun is leaving Harry wondering what I have on him."

"He doesn't know?" EJ asks.

I shake my head as I slowly pull the paper from my cupcake. I like to take my time whenever I eat an Ed cupcake. Part of it is because I don't eat many of them, because I'd weigh six hundred pounds if I consumed as many of them as I truly wanted. But the other reason, the most important reason of all, is because Ed made them, and that makes them the best cupcakes in the world. Also, there was a little tiny part of me that hoped he was thinking about me when he made them. Even better if he baked them while naked.

My eyes slide closed as I bite into the little treat and moan. The tart lemon, with a hint of sour cream, along with the super sweet strawberry frosting, danced over my taste buds.

"Good lord, get a room," EJ says.

My eyes pop open and I realize that both of my friends are watching me. I swallow, then reach for my coffee.

"What?"

"You sound like you're having sex with your cupcake," Savannah says. "Just ask him out already."

I sniff. "I have no idea what you're talking about."

"Sweetie, please, we know you're still in love with Ed," EJ says.

My face heats. "I'm not in love with him."

Sure, I told them more than once about my crush, but

there's no reason for my friends to know that I am neck deep in love and going under for the third time. Or that I think a lot about his…frosting.

"It's the cupcake and that's it."

I glare them both into silence, then pick up my cupcake and start to eat it again. Nothing is going to dampen my experience with my treat.

Get Delicious TODAY—> One-click

ACKNOWLEDGMENTS

As I always say, no book is written by just me. I spend hours working with editors, author friends, and family getting this thing to where I want it to be.

Thanks to Heidi Shoham and Noel Varner for kicking my arse and getting this book into shape. Thanks to my husband Les and our ever suffering daughters—including our dog daughter Maisy who is sick of me taking pics of her for insta—for helping me deal with this book longer than I should.

Outside of my family there are always two people who hear of my work first, and that is Brandy Walker and Joy Harris. Ladies, thanks aways for advice and letting me bitch to you.

And thanks of course to the rest of my support apparatus, The Addicts and all my other readers out there. Thanks to your support, I have a career I love.

THE MELISSA SCHROEDER INSTALOVE COLLECTION

SAME WORLD. ANY ORDER. INDIVIDUAL LOVE.

Introducing the Melissa Schroeder Instalove Collection. All books are in the same world but can be read in any order as they are stand alones. All books are low on drama, high on heat, and a have happily ever after. Look for the Instalove stamp whenever you want a short, fun, sexy story.

ABOUT THE AUTHOR

From an early age, USA Today Bestselling author Melissa loved to read. When she discovered the romance genre, she started to listen to the voices in her head. After years of following her AF Major husband around, she is happy to be settled in Northern Virginia surrounded by horses, wineries, and many, many Wegmans.

Keep up with Mel, her releases, and her appearances by subscribing to her NEWSLETTER or join in the fun with her Harmless Addicts!

Check out all her other books, family trees and other info at her website!
If you would want contact Mel, email her at:
melissa@melissaschroeder.net

- instagram.com/melschro
- amazon.com/author/melissa_schroeder
- facebook.com/MelissaSchroederfanpage
- twitter.com/melschroeder
- bookbub.com/authors/melissa-schroeder
- goodreads.com/Melissa_Schroeder

ALSO BY MELISSA SCHROEDER

The Camos and Cupcakes World

- Camos and Cupcakes
- The Fillmore Siblings
- Juniper Springs-coming soon

Melissa Schroeder's Instalove Collection

- Dominion Rockstar Romance
- Mafia Sisters
- Faking It
- The Fighting Sullivans
- Single Titles

The Santini World

- The Santinis
- Semper Fi Marines
- The Fitzpatricks

The Harmless World

- The Harmless Series
- A Little Harmless Military Romance
- Task Force Hawaii

Check out the rest of Mel's books by:

- Interest
- Series
- Entire Backlist